Plutonic

A Novella

Paula C. Deckard

Library and Archives Canada

Plutonic / Paula C. Deckard

ISBN (paperback) 978-0-9959574-8-0
e-Book ISBN 978-0-9959574-7-3

Edited By Sam Whittam

Cover art by Neda Aria

FOR LAURA

"I think she always nursed a small mad hope"

-       *John Shade*
Pale Fire (V. Nabokov, 1962)

In my mind, she either suffocated or slit her wrists. Or she drowned to honour the dreams that I'd shared with her. She had never gone into details about how she would do it, except that she had researched it to the dot. September is known to be suicide awareness month, where some people will voluntarily touch the point of the Grim Reaper's scythe, saving him the work of coming for them. There is something poetic about killing yourself during autumn, given it's your favourite time of the year. It's when you take one last glance at the beautiful landscape that has always brought joy to you until your last string of hope becomes so thin it snaps, and you realise that you've been deluding yourself all this time. But it was worth it.

I received my last email from Sandra a few weeks before she "stepped out of life," as her dad had put it. Her mental health had deteriorated, and she was writing to me from a mental health institution. I thought she was on a spiritual cleansing journey, making progress in healing and looking to do a master's degree in sociology. Instead, she told me that a misogynist ghost was haunting her, and she thought of what it felt like to be loved by it, as she believed that he never did love her. Had that ghost not stepped into Sandra's life and stopped her from killing herself too early, she and I would have never met. Perhaps it would have been better that way. I never understood why she wanted me to know who that ghost was. Perhaps to build some cosmic connection—a sick love triangle. Or perhaps she wanted me to meet my evil twin to gain some balance.

Sandra Williams and I knew each other for less than a year; we met at a backpacker's hostel in Reykjavik and became inseparable. I remember her entering the girls' dorm with a smile that looked like she had been looking for me. She said she was allocated a top bunk and asked if it was OK to place her backpack next to mine. What struck me as a surprise and coincidence was that she was from Leeds, and I was from Manchester.

Leeds University had been my first choice university, but I didn't get in. It had eliminated all hope that I had at the time. Instead, I graduated from a college outside of London and returned to Manchester because I couldn't afford to live in Central London, nor could I find a decent job. Renting my parents' flat in the Northern Quarter was cheaper and more bearable than being in a messy houseshare with people.

After suffering from a mental breakdown, Sandra became a Leeds dropout. Later she told me she was suicidal and had even set a date for January of that year to end things. Obviously, she was still standing, but not for long.

The story began long before the trip to Reykjavik. It wasn't even a dream destination of mine. When I was in between jobs, I decided to focus on some personal and freelance journalist work concerning the city I lived in. I was greatly inspired by the Humans of New York photoblog and started a similar online journal for Manchester and surrounding areas. My main focus was on trauma, which was something I could always detect in a person's eyes. I despised being the centre of attention myself, so my website never carried a headshot photograph of me. Rather, each Instagram and Facebook post would be about a specific person and their story. Sometimes I was so intrigued by the person I would do a short video special that involved specific interview questions. It typically became the story or highlight of the month. I caught the local press's attention and piqued their interest in their residents. Some even invited me to attend a formal face-to-face interview, but I declined; instead, I agreed to an email interview with Manchester Metro News since it seemed most relevant to what I was doing. The Evening News featured a small story based on one of my subjects' stories because they were a local victim and survivor of predatory stalking. I wasn't proud of that mention because they made my subject look like a caricature, as though her life story didn't matter, nor did it affect anyone. Suddenly with over ten thousand people on my mailing list, I felt like giving up. People requested to be interviewed and featured without understanding that it wasn't how I worked. I chose my interviewees by approaching them in the café, at the bar, or in the library because it required me to step out of my comfort zone. I didn't want them to know who I was, as it entailed too much bias. Whenever I failed because I wasn't able to build mutual trust, I would be heartbroken. Some had come crawling back after realising who I was, but it was too late for them to be in my spotlight.

I incorporated polls, so I didn't have to evaluate what people wanted to read or see by reading all incoming emails. You couldn't expect too much from a one-girl army who sucked at making Patreon work as a sole income source.

JAKE

My last interviewee before I took off to Iceland was Jake Carradine, whom I picked up at the club and slept with. I was ovulating and horny, so I hung out at Satan's Hollow, which was the only decent rock club left in town. If I wasn't to get laid, I had to dance it out and make love to music that I enjoyed. Besides sex, dancing was the only form of bodily expression that granted me freedom. The occasional jog would do the job, too, until it got boring.

Satan's Hollow was full of adolescents, but I blended in all right, even though I was more than twice their age. All I had to do was wear black and let my Asian features shine through. I didn't think I'd find anyone interesting or have sex at all that night until I met Jake. He came alone and looked perplexed when he entered the hall as though he'd expected to discover something different. He was dressed like a biker in that black leather jacket with a white T-shirt underneath. But I judged people by their shoes, and he was wearing red All-Stars, which made him a musician. Looking lost for a second, he walked to the bar and ordered a Bacardi Breezer. I had claimed the corner booth for myself, where I was watching a bunch of fifteen-year-old mosher girls eyeing Jake, giggling. When he turned around to check the half-empty dancefloor, the young girls in the booth waved him over, but he courteously declined with a half-wave and smile. When he came up to me, I pretended not to notice and sipped my cranberry juice. When he pointed at the other end of my booth, I shrugged a shoulder. Sitting across from me now, he held out a hand.

"I stopped shaking hands in 2020," I said.

"Oh, sure."

He took a nervous sip of his drink and said, "I'm Jakob."

"Diane."

He smiled and seemed relieved. For a second, he reminded me of Lenny Kravitz; perhaps he was also half Bahamian. Jakob looked like he was my age, perhaps a bit younger. His microlocs were medium-length and had loose ends because they weren't cut properly, but I liked it.

"I thought a gig was on tonight?" he asked in a mild Lancs accent.

"It got cancelled so it's club night."

He nodded understandingly. "So the bellend at the door had me pay for a club night. Wanker."

He seemed kind of stupid but cute and was the only guy in that room who wasn't wearing eyeliner. He didn't need any; his eyelashes were naturally long and curly. His beauty came easily and made me jealous, which was reason enough for me to want him because I couldn't see through his hazel eyes. And there was his dark past.

"Do you come here often?" he said.

Had anybody else said it, it would have been a pick-up line, but he appeared to be very unsure about that place.

"No, but I used to go to Jilly's Rockworld every weekend."

His eyes lit up, and I saw shiny white teeth brightening up the room. He leaned forward and began telling me about going to Jilly's, too, before it closed down in 2010. He and his first band used to play there a lot. I didn't attend many gigs back in the day, but I would be there during club nights on Fridays and Saturdays, hiding out in the basement. That was where they played emo, screamo, and some metal, while the top floor had a lot of monotonous and repetitive darkwave and electro music that attracted most of the crowd.

Soon we started chatting about our favourite band—Joy Divison, and he was already in love. But mutual interest in music doesn't mean anything.

He offered to buy me a drink, but I declined. Instead, I leaned forward and marvelled at his eyelashes, then studied his manly hands.

"Can I interview you?"

We were walking towards his flat in Hulme, where I insisted on taking a portrait of him in front of the Arch Bridge. It turned out to be a beautiful shot, with the street lights illuminating the background and the 365 tonnes of steel.

The moment he closed his door behind us, he pressed me against it and kissed me with a hand around my throat. He had an earthy smell, blended with clove and sweet tobacco leaf.

Politely, I pushed him back and reminded him of the interview.

"You weren't kidding, eh?"

He was wrong to think that I used the interview request as a pretext to fuck him. It was highly important to keep all interviews unbiased. I needed that level of distance to do my job right. Everybody knew that sex would ruin everything, and that was exactly what I loved about it, except I knew how to build some tension. Seeing how serious I was about it, he prepped us chamomile tea to calm the nerves, but he insisted on being a memorable one, so I'd never forget about it. Before I knew it, he took off all his clothes except for his socks. He leaned back in his reclining chair and looked at me.

"As long as I answer your questions, it doesn't matter how I look, does it?"

When staring at his broad, trained shoulders and upper arms, my gaze wandered towards his half-erect penis that was resting on his muscular quad.

Give me a short summary of who you and your parents are.

"My name is Jakob Carradine, born and bred in Manchester. My father is half-Cuban and half-Bahamian, and my mother is English. We moved from Lancs to Manchester when I was a toddler. My parents believed there would be more job opportunities and tolerance in the city after the recession in the 1980s. Dad found a job as a forklift operator and gradually worked his way up from there. It took him almost twenty years to become a logistics manager and earn twenty-five per cent of company shares. My mum is a piano teacher and got me into music, but she doesn't like my style of music. She has no ear for complicated blues or easy three-chord punk, not to mention sexy R&B or technical metal. That said, I play in a mainstream indie band. Occasionally, I wish I played the guitar like John Frusciante."

What's your earliest childhood memory?

"I was five when my parents and I went on a holiday together. We took a road trip down south. My dad wanted to see the maritime heritage in Southampton, and on the way, my mum wanted to stop in Stonehenge. I remember being very happy because they were young and in love. As a child, you can feel that wonderful energy. And whenever there was tension, I would summon my imaginary friend Kenny, who was a shapeshifter. Just before we arrived at Stonehenge on a busy day, we were stuck in traffic. Dad was impatient behind the wheel and wanted to skip it, calling the monument a hoax and a waste of time. It got Mum upset. We still went, but they didn't talk. We were all disappointed to find out that the monument was fenced off, and we couldn't enter the circle. But Kenny disobeyed. I saw him hiding behind the rocks. He was wearing bloody animal skins. I don't remember how I got in, but I was suddenly inside the circle with Kenny, surrounded by those ancient rocks. Apparently, I was reported missing for two hours. Just as the police arrived, I showed up in front of the fence wearing Kenny's animal skins. Up to this day, I don't remember what happened. But the rest of our road trip was a blast."

Tell me something that has had a huge impact on your life.

"Music has always had a huge impact on me; it's there when I need it the most. I could be in a near-death experience, of which there have been many, and still find my way back into the real world. I was sexually abused and raped at thirteen, but the strange thing was that I didn't think much of it.

I was raised as a devout Catholic boy who has always put the family first. My mum used to send me to my dying grandmother, who had trouble acknowledging me as a black grandchild. My dad never bothered trying to bond with her, but my mother didn't want her mother to die without knowing her only grandchild. Every week I had to bring Nana lunch and spend hours reading the Daily Mail to her. I always felt like washing my mouth afterwards.

One time, she asked me to take off my clothes and wash my privates. I did as told, but she didn't provide me a towel to dry off, so I slipped on her waxed linoleum flooring, hit my head, and fell unconscious. I woke up on my stomach with my right cheek pressed hard against the floor. My behind was lifted, and she was penetrating my arse with her walking stick.

I didn't tell my parents; instead, I went to Connie, a schoolmate who had a crush on me. I didn't like her back, but I had to recover what was left of me somehow, so I stole her virginity.

When I went to see Nana a week later, I found her dead, hanging naked in her walk-in bathtub with a satin scarf wrapped around her neck. The other end was tied to the shower head. I found all sorts of kinky clothing in her dresser, so I grabbed a pair of the nurse's vinyl gloves and started playing Stadium Arcadium. It was time to make some art.

I put eyeshadow, red lipstick, and rouge on her before dressing her up with fishnet stockings and gloves. She had a black dildo which I had a hard time shoving up her arse, so I just rammed it inside her dry cunt. I sat with her for a long time— for as long as it took to forgive her. I was analysing her pale, wrinkly skin and thick toenails. It was difficult to believe that I had her DNA. I didn't bother closing her bloodshot eyes, which were staring at nothing at all. The song *Wet Sand* was playing in the background, and by the time it finished, I left."

I stopped recording and walked over to him. Jake looked totally complacent, with both hands folded and resting on his abs. I unbuttoned my black jeans, pulled them down, and took off my Sex Pistols T-shirt. He leaned forward, placed a hand on my bruised inner thigh, and glided upward. His microlocs had frayed more at the end.

ADAM

One day, a local podcaster named Adam reached out to me via social media and invited me to attend his show. His podcast was called Intrepid Urban Fox, which featured a vast range of dark topics revolving around local occurrences and social issues. He made you question people and their statuses and motives, calling them conformists deluded enough to hope for a better life. We are made to trust authoritative figures by design, but what really went on behind closed doors? If you had a million dollars, would you really give a shit about anyone else in need? Doesn't everyone have ulterior motives? I was rather intimidated by some of the episodes I listened to and almost declined the invite.

I was on the phone with Adam, providing me with some questions in advance because I asked for them. He was polite and courteous, but I noticed some cocky undertones when I said I had one condition—no video. We already had a date set, and Adam kept trying to change my mind. But I made it clear to him that that wasn't happening.

I knew he was dying to find out what I looked like, and it wouldn't surprise me if he reached out to some of my interviewees to find out. Luckily, all my life, I'd kept a low profile despite my journalistic background. You wouldn't even find me in any high school yearbooks.

On the day of the interview, he called me early on Skype; he sounded defeated but remained reserved. He had his video on, showing off his handsome face that reminded me of a British version of Mark Hoppus with a less round head but a determinedly sharp jawline. He had gunmetal blue or hazel blue eyes (I couldn't tell, and it annoyed me), short brown hair, and a broad forehead.

"Hiya love, how are you? I can't see you."

"You don't like my default picture?" I said.

"No, I don't. It's not real-time," he said with a half grin. "Nice legs, though."

My default depicted me holding my Nikon camera closely against my face, cradling the lens. My upper body was bent downward, as though photographing a manhole cover, which I was. A broken piece of mirror was right on top of it. I was wearing shorts. I interviewed a bum named Joseph that day. He was later found dead by bin men. I had gone to see Joseph again when the owner at the off-license told me the story, saying Joseph was beaten to death. He was the one who found Joseph behind the store's rubbish bin at the back of the building. No newspaper had cared to write about that former teacher who slept with a sixteen-year-old pupil and lost his job and wife. It was the little slut who drugged him and lured him to the back of the school's canteen, where she raped him. I wanted to share that story on the podcast, telling Mancunians they were turning a blind eye to murder. I couldn't help but feel responsible for his death, even though he secretly had a death wish. Had I put him and his story in the spotlight and made him more vulnerable? Ever since that story started circulating, I noticed more trolls on my social media.

"Are you going to hit record?" I asked Adam.

"What's the rush?" he said with a broad smile. "Have you got anything planned for today?"

"What if I said yes?"

"I'm sorry," he said with a resentful grin. "You have to forgive me for being so curious."

He put on his Joe Rogan-style headphones and seemed to be getting ready.

The pod went for two hours, which had felt like more. Occasionally, he would tease and flirt, asking what type of guys I liked to date and whether I would have picked him for an interview if I had seen him in the library. The truth was I didn't know. Though he'd done his best to remain professional with me, I didn't feel like pointing out his *faux pas*. He seemed to be this way with everyone. I couldn't say whether I cared about gaining more followers after the show or not. After all, his audience was different from mine.

SANDRA AND I

A day before I took off, I posted Jake's story. I sent out a newsletter stating that it was the last story for a little while. If anyone cared, they could follow my Instagram for Reykjavik updates. Jake's story got instant likes and comments on my social channel. Usually, there was a fair bit for me to cut or edit after the transcription process because the subject asked to take out specific details. Afterwards, I had them sign a consent form; in return, I'd sign a confidentiality agreement. Some people didn't want their full name stated, or they wanted a pseudonym. However, all stories and photographs were one hundred per cent real. Signing forms was never necessary at first until the press approached me. You can't trust people, after all. Some female commenters claimed Jake was their ex and wanted to know how I knew him, but I did not interact. They became aggressive and asked whether I'd fucked him.

I felt much lighter on the plane, leaving the country that had become a mess a long time ago. The news revolved around floods in Liverpool; a huge part of the outskirts was underwater. What made me sad was that the entire stretch of Ainsdale Beach and Southport Beach was no more.

At least I had my subjects nearby. When not listening to music, I'd listen to my subjects talk. That was my kind of audiobook. I had over seventy interviews on my iPod. Depending on my mood, I loved listening to the most recent ones, such as Jake's. I had only ever slept with two interviewees and home-wrecked one because I was stupidly besotted like Annik Honoré.

When listening to Jake, I couldn't help but replay our sexual encounter—how he almost choked me unconscious while sodomising me without warning. Before falling asleep, I remember gazing at the dark brown of his irises that were swirling around his pupils like whirlwinds. I couldn't tell if he was sucking me into a wormhole or a black hole because I didn't know the difference. Were we travelling to a different universe, or were we dying? The weird thing was that the sex was exactly how I had imagined it to be after a precognitive encounter.

Jake had asked me to leave out that part about not having had his concussion treated. When I said he hadn't brought up the concussion, he said, never mind. He ended up with post-concussive syndrome that affected his sleep. During the phases of not sleeping, he experienced personality changes.

Upon arrival, I took a shuttle to the hostel. The low-hanging clouds stretched across the entire city like a bunch of dust bunnies that had found one another in the sky. I couldn't tell if the clouds in Manchester or Reykjavik were worse. The lobby was full of young backpackers from all over the world. The English accents ranged from Australian to Zimbabwean, whereas the races were mainly Caucasian and Far East Asian. But I didn't want to mingle.

I arrived one hour early for check-in, but luckily housekeeping was done, so they let me go to my room. I chose the girls' dorm because they were typically cleaner and quieter. Had I been ten years younger, I wouldn't have minded being in the mixed dorm. The pillow was soft, and the sheets were clean. When the smell of petrichor hit my nostrils, and the first raindrops hit the ground, I fell into a deep slumber.

The giant wave was back. It had grown in size and was closer than before. Why was it taking its time? Perhaps because I was taking too much time doing the right thing to pass the time. One of my favourite scenes in Deep Impact was where Téa Leoni's character and her father hugged seconds before the tidal wave wiped out the city. What scared me the most about disaster movies was that I'd be on my own and fatherless. No one would care about putting my subjects in a safe place for the next generation of Mancunians to discover.

I woke to a gentle turn of the doorknob.

Sandra and I checked out the local sights in the afternoon. Even though we were starving, we decided to skip the coffee shop, where coffee and croissants would have cost us over ten quid per person. Instead, we found better deals at the local supermarket. Sitting in front of that huge, plain concrete church, we ate our soup and bread like two skint runaways. It had felt like whiling away the hours with a long-lost sister whom I'd never met but always knew existed. She was honest with me within the first few hours of hanging out. It took her a lot of courage to admit it, and she was so anxious she couldn't even finish her soup.

"I already knew who you were before we met," she said.

For a second, she had me stumped. I thought about my social media posts: besides the trolls, did I make myself vulnerable to stalkers as well? Should I have shared posts about my whereabouts?

She continued, "I listened to your podcast episode the other week."

"You did," I said and instantly lost my appetite.

"I was very touched by Joseph's story because I knew Brittany Savory."

"Who's Brittany?"

"His rapist."

I dropped my piece of bread.

"We went to the same high school in Wakefield. During the last year of sixth form, she moved to Manchester. It didn't surprise me that she hadn't changed. She had an affair with a PE teacher, which was so cliché. When it came out, he got fired. Rumours had it that he wanted it to end, but she wouldn't let him and threatened to tell his fiancée."

"What happened to the teacher."

"He killed himself."

I hated it when people talked about "killing oneself" without being more specific. Did they stick their head inside a gas oven? Did they overmedicate? Did they hang themselves? Did they crash into a tree?

She said, "What fascinated me about Joseph was that he didn't even get involved with Brittany from the start. But knowing that she didn't take rejections well, I wasn't surprised to hear what she did."

I had nothing to say except that it was interesting to hear a background story relevant to my subject's original story. It made me wonder whether I should do prequel stories, but I instantly dropped that thought. Prequels or sequels ruin a story's uniqueness. It's like franchising a movie for the sake of profit.

"About fifteen years ago," Sandra began, "there was a young British girl and her family who went on holiday to Turkey. There, she met a seventeen-year-old German boy who was a virgin. She lured him to her hotel room and seduced him. He got so nervous that he instantly came the moment she touched his dick. Do you know what happened to him?"

"He was charged with sexual abuse of a minor and spent almost a year in a Turkish prison."

"So you know that story?" she asked.

"It was all over the Manchester Evening News in 2007. How do you know about it? You were only four, Sandra."

I didn't mean to be patronising, but I couldn't help snapping at her and shutting her up. She had brought up a time in my past that suddenly flashed before me. I remember following the case of that German boy and empathising with him. I also remember hating that girl's guts and her mother even more so. The boy was innocent, and a gynaecological examination proved it. Still, he sat in prison because of a lying thirteen-year-old bitch that claimed to be fifteen. I remember those large panda bear eyes and emo fringes. Barely any of those girls had lips, either.

The silence between Sandra and me lasted for a while, and I could tell she felt slightly guilty and ashamed.

"I want you to know that I do not have any ulterior motives for meeting you, Diane. There is something warm and soothing about you. And something else that I can't figure out. I haven't told many people, but when I sense a deep connection with someone, I have to pursue it. It's rare, but it's the only thing that keeps me going. And trust me, there hasn't even been a handful of people yet."

Suddenly she gulped down the remaining lukewarm soup, now holding an empty paper cup. She burped and let out a hiccup at the same time, and we both laughed.

We joined a hostel event on our first night, where the hosts took us to an indoor axe-throwing place. For a slender lady, five-foot and five inches, Sandra had quite the strength; she even aimed well for a first-timer. It wasn't physical strength—

more like a forced adrenaline rush or controlled survival instinct. In fact, she scared me. Despite her gentleness, she looked like she was capable of killing someone when she had to.

Everyone was drinking except for the two of us. Though Sandra was tempted, I reminded her of her meds. I acted like the older sister because I never had anyone to boss around, and it became naturally instinctual. Furthermore, she reminded me of a younger version of myself. She didn't seem to mind it either. Later I found out that she'd experienced a lot more shit than I did at twenty, but she was still able to lay bare a high level of innocence. I knew from the moment I met her that she would be the most loyal person I'd ever know. But what drew her so close to me was still a mystery to me.

I rented a car so we could head to the Sky Lagoon hot springs without relying on overpriced tour guides to take us there. On our way, Sandra insisted on examining my natal chart. After gathering all the details of my birth, she spent a long time putting together a report.

"You believe in this shit, don't you?"

"Of course," she said.

"But the principles of astrology are based on the night sky from over 2000 years ago. The stars' positions and configurations change every century, Sandra."

"You're right," she said. "But the remnants stay relevant. Plus, it's all about the small details, not the generic descriptions you read on the last page of a newspaper."

The salty scent of the Atlantic Ocean was mesmerising even when intermingled with sulphur. The breathtaking view of the faraway horizon and surrounding rock formations made you feel like you were in the middle of the ocean. Geothermal waters have always fascinated me. Those places are closer to the earth's core than anything. You'll always stay warm in the earth's crust, as though in your mother's womb. Once you're out, you're cold and doomed for as long as it takes to return to where you came from.

We were both wearing bikinis when we came out of the changing rooms. That was when I noticed those wrist scars on her. It wasn't just a few razor cuts here and there, but her lower arm was marked with a six-inch keloid scar. It looked like she had slashed it with a knife less than six months ago. She also had a tree branch tattooed on her right arm and a flower on her right Achilles tendon.

We had to rinse ourselves first before stepping into the hot spring, during which she asked me to hold her hand. The steam and the hot water instantly cleared my senses, and I suddenly re-experienced Jake's first touch. Sandra and I moved away from the crowd and explored every corner of the infinity pool. She appeared to be very happy, and for some reason, it struck me that she was rarely like that and that it was a special moment. Her long brown hair, naturally curly, and her large brown eyes resembled those of a ten-year-old who knew no evil. But her lips—her lips told me otherwise. Her lower lip was slightly fuller than the top one, and she'd had to smile each time to ensure people she was content or happy. Still, every facial expression brought upon a sadness or pain that, even when her lips curled into a genuine smile, she couldn't conceal it. It was as though she was marked with something bad a very long time ago, and she couldn't overcome or defeat it. The saddening part of it all was that she knew.

"Tell me," I said. "What did you discover in my natal chart that you're so eager to share?"

Her eyes sparkled, and she moved closer to me, looking me deeply in the eyes. The steam behind her rose and dissipated in the air.

"You have a lot of water in your chart, Diane," she said. "You need a stable emotional life for your well-being. You're balancing it well with the creative things you're doing. You might think you have no more emotions left, but the truth is that you're regulating them with your art. However, you were born under the first-quarter moon, which means that you have to overcome many challenges. Nothing will come easily during personal growth. At least you have Virgo as your ascendant, who gives you analytical capabilities and efficiency, which is what everybody sees on the surface. It keeps you in check."

"I'm sorry, hun," I said and swam away from her. "There's a little too much bias in what you just said."

"Why? Because you told me about you?" She seemed amused. "I'm just connecting the dots!

You can be as ignorant or rational as you want, but in this case, I'm afraid you'll have to live with that. But there is something else that's important."

She caught up to me and said, "Hades moon."

"What?"

"You have an intense emotional energy brooding inside of you, a lot of anger, to be exact. It defines the karmic pattern in your life due to an excess of plutonic energies."

"OK, OK. What?"

She kissed me in that instant. It was the kind of kiss you would give your lover when they were leaving you to go somewhere far, far away. It took my breath away. There was a mild patchouli scent emanating from her hair, combined with sulphur and other minerals. Her soft lips tasted youthful, like the ones of a nineteen-year-old boy, but a lot more epiphanic. Then, she looked at me as though something bad would happen any minute.

"I'm worried about you," she said. How she talked to me made me feel like time was running out, but not mine.

"I can't tell whether you're weird or insane."

"I prefer insightful," she said. "You see, your Neptune is in my twelfth house, which means we have a strong spiritual connection…"

"OK, shut the fuck up."

On the drive back to the hostel, she told me about the god of the underworld—Hades, which was partly interesting until she started babbling about my Scorpio moon in conjunction with Pluto. Then, my Mercury and Venus square Pluto. I had a phase during which I was interested in astronomy and studied the surrounding planets, but I never cared enough about the dwarf planet. All I knew was that its atmosphere was full of toxic carbon monoxide and volatile nitrogen. Astrology, on the other hand, was something I gave up on many years ago.

Sandra asked if I knew about Pluto's heart-shaped ice plain on the surface. I said no. The clouds were hanging low over the outskirts of Reykjavik, but the setting sun was painting a warm, bright orange surface above the horizon.

"There is a reason for frozen hearts. And thawing them could take years, especially when you are so far away from the sun," she said.

*

I got closer to her in three days than I did with most friends in twenty years. Twenty—That was how old she was when we met, and there was me in my mid-thirties. Her half-naive and half-mature sides would be the most confusing aspects of her personality. Yet, the love she spread was genuine, and there would be moments I wanted to break her to see if she could still stand afterwards. She never shared with me specific details of her past: the apparent rape in her childhood or begging her ex to kill her, which he almost did. And I wish he had, as I wouldn't have veered off course in my life that I once had perfectly under control before her. She was horribly fate-driven, even though she would deny it. Since I already had the urge to break her, I didn't want to know how other people in her life felt towards her, especially the wrong kind of people. We texted each other almost daily, and she would write me long emails at least once a week for the next few months. Despite being only one hour away from each other, neither of us made an effort to visit the other. During that time, she was going through a series of lows with the occasional delusional ups. She told me about having gone to see a palm reader, whom she didn't tell anything about her past but who immediately knew about her short-lived karmic relationship with her ex. Apparently, the palmist gave her a sad look when she left.

BEFORE I DROWN

"I can't stop thinking about your soft skin," Jake texted me.

I never called him after the release of his story, but it didn't mean I wasn't thinking of his body, his story, or the long eyelashes.

Jake invited me to his band's gig at the Academy, but I was hesitant about going. It didn't matter in which hall they would be playing, the Academy brought both bad and good memories. I had no desire to go there. He said I was the only one he'd put on the guest list and that he wouldn't do it for anyone else. His band was the second support act before the main band that I didn't even like. I decided to see his band by skipping the first and main acts. I knew the type of crowd that would be there. With the intention of not standing out, I wore black and kept my hood on. I even overdid my eye makeup, which didn't look good with my almond-shaped eyes. I also put on my lip ring piercing, which I hadn't worn in a year.

Sandra was worried about my involvement with Jake and told me to be careful because the trolling over Jake's story never stopped. She didn't have much to say about Jake except that he had a dark aura (judging by my hot photograph at the Arch Bridge), and she didn't think I was safe with him. There was also a slight jealous undertone in her voice when we last spoke on the phone.

My limbs froze when I arrived at the Academy. It had been a few years since I last attended concerts there, but I wasn't much of a concert-goer anymore. A line of mosher kids stretched around the building during intermission, just like they did back in 2002. I should've come when a live act was playing, so fewer people would be hanging out outside, staring around, trying to spot famous people they could fuck or give a blowjob to. I remember witnessing American pop punk bands sleeping with underage emo girls who wore thick side-swept fringes, and all looked like seventeen with those thick layers of makeup. Underneath, they were all just *thick* and hopeless.

Despite looking similar to them that night, I was stared down, so I decided to put on a face mask as I entered the halls. Jake's band would come on in about twenty minutes.

I walked past a tall girl who shouldered me aside on purpose and didn't look back to say a word. She had long, straight blond hair and wore red faux leather pants and a black hoodie like mine. As my gaze went down, I noticed black-heeled combat boots that would make her five inches taller than she really was.

I didn't get a proper look at her face, but judging by her posture, she was slightly older than the rest. I watched her approach a man who seemed to be a roadie or sound guy, judging by his earplugs and the cables he was carrying around. They kissed each other on the cheek and started talking.

I ignored it and simply rushed to the main hall to find a safe corner away from the crowd. The left side of the stage was typically the most favourable place for me to hide. The centre had too much moshing going on, whereas the right side was reserved for hysterical girls to be close to the "hot" guitarist. That said, not all bands had a hot guitarist, but I knew that, in this case, they did.

The same guy with the cables appeared on stage to finish setting up the instruments, and I suddenly felt like someone was eying me from the right. When the light dimmed more, I moved back a few rows. My hands were shaking when Jake and his band climbed the stage and waved at the cheering crowd. He had the exact same outfit on from when I first met him, except that he was also wearing a beige-black Telecaster around his body. He scanned the crowd from left to right and spotted me right away despite the hood and face mask. He winked. The rest of the band wasn't all that fashion-conscious with their tight black jeans and torn shirts. Though the frontman and singer had similar features to Jarvis Cocker, there wasn't anything spectacular about their performance or music. Being in the crowd was like conforming to the movements of a hot wave that you couldn't control. You had to be a part of it, and I hated it. At some point during the show, I moved all the way to the back. Sandra had texted me, asking how the gig was, but I had no motivation to reply.

Jake bent his guitar strings like John Frusciante, but he couldn't create the clean, controlled tones with his fuzz pedal as John did. He was still good, just not in a way that would maintain my attraction to him. Just as they announced their last song, I moved to the exit and decided to leave. I was there for only forty-five minutes, but it had felt like three hours.

When I stepped outside, I pulled the mask off my face and took a deep breath of the hot August air. Oxford Road was busy for a Tuesday night, and there was no safe opportunity to jaywalk to the other side.

"Hey, bitch!"

That female voice sounded a lot closer than I thought. The thought of being followed didn't occur to me due to all that traffic noise. As I stopped and turned, someone struck my head with an empty bottle. I didn't hear the sound of shattering glass; instead, I heard a loud clunk and felt numbness on the left side of my forehead. My vision blurred, and another clunking sound occurred when the bottle hit the ground. It didn't break. A couple of men were holding her back, and all I saw were fake red leather pants.

"Stay the fuck away from Jake, you cunt," was all I heard behind me as I chose to walk away from that noise. Some people surrounded me, asking if I was OK and if I needed an ambulance. The blow to the head had happened so fast that it felt like someone was waking me from a distant dream.

"Where did you go?" Jake asked me on the phone as I was still walking home. I chose to walk via Gay Village because I've always experienced the least amount of discrimination there. My vision was still blurry, but at least I knew the area inside out, so I was still able to navigate through certain structures.

"I'm heading home, Jake," I said while pressing hard against that huge, painful bump on my forehead.

"Are you crying? What's going on?"

I spotted the Alan Turing memorial and sat on the bench next to the statue to catch some breath while pressing my bump against the cold bronze. The pain instantly subsided, and Jake's voice became just noise.

"What, what?" I said.

"I said: What the fuck happened, Diane?"

He sounded like a concerned boyfriend for a second, but none of them ever were. They just needed to know who did you harm and then had to boost their ego by retaliating.

"Someone struck me in the head," I said.

"Fuck, are you ok? Where are you now?"

"Yeah. I'm almost home," I said as things got blurry again, as though I was about to lose consciousness this time.

"Who did this?"

"The bitch in the fake red leather pants."

The other line went dead.

The navy blue wave was closer than ever, within arm's reach. But something was strange about it; it wasn't moving. Why would time stop like that? That wave was supposed to wash me away, along with all the memories and impurities that emerged from the surface of my chest. A sudden rage grew within me, and I began kicking it. That was when I noticed that my foot went right through the still-standing water. Carefully, I reached my hand through the cold mass of water and stepped through the wave. I entered a room that had a dome-shaped ceiling illustrating the stars that I'd last observed at the planetarium in Greenwich. The surrounding walls were made of ocean water. Beneath the centre of the dome was Sandra, sitting on her knees with her eyes closed.

I kneeled in front of her and shook her. "Sandra! What are you doing here?"

I wasn't worried; I was pissed because it was my realm, my ending. She showed no reaction, and when I looked up at the stars, they were no longer there. Instead, it looked like we were at the bottom of a huge pool, looking up. A mini shark swam above us, causing the surface lights to flicker. The water was not coming down to fill this place.

"Get out, Sandra!" I shouted at her. "I don't want you here!"

There might have been a tear running down her cheek, but I didn't care. It began to rain as though we were in a sail riding through a storm. Whatever shield was holding back the seawater was starting to break—both walls and ceiling. Water was leaking through various cracks, filling the space. The flickering surface light was dimming faster by the second. I curled my arms under Sandra's armpits and dragged her to the wall where I came from, hoping there was enough time to pull her out of that space. As I reached the wall, I heard a crack above us, and it looked like a roaring waterfall after snowmelt was about to hit us.

Someone snapped their fingers in front of me, but I didn't want to open my eyes. Things felt like they were spinning around me, even with my eyes closed.

"Hiya luv, are you all right?"

I suddenly realised that I had never made it home. I was still sitting next to Alan Turing, resting my head on his shoulder, which was the hardest pillow I'd ever slept on.

I opened my eyes to a man in a polo shirt. When I sat straight, he scrunched up his face while pointing at my bump.

"What motherfucker would do that to a woman?" he said.

"Another woman," I murmured.

Another guy behind him held my phone, which I must have dropped. He said, "I'm sorry, there've been two calls, and I answered them both."

"From who?"

"The first one was Jakob. He's on his way."

"Fuck."

"The second one was Sandra. She said to stay with you and call her when you wake up. So, I'm gonna do that."

From a distance, I already saw Sandra's name on the dial. When trying to grab the phone off of him, he held out a strict hand and said, "Let me tell your loved ones that you're OK, all right?"

The guy in the polo shirt stepped in between to examine my bump. He pressed hard against it, which sent a stinging pain all the way down my spine.

"You must ice it, luv."

The other guy handed me back my phone, and I saw that Sandra was still on the other line.

"Are you OK?" I said.

"No, what? Are *you* OK?"

"There was so much water, Sandra. I thought we were going to die!" I said it with a decent level of reservedness and focus so these guys wouldn't deem me insane. Despite giving me a funny look, they soon got distracted by something else. Their eyes grew in size as they pointed behind me. One of them mouthed a "Wow!"

I could already smell the sweet scent of tobacco leaf and sandalwood before Jake stepped forward and kneeled before Alan Turing and me. His hand touched my face, whereas the other one examined my bump. From my peripherals, I could see the two lads swooning over the scene or merely because Jake was hotter than anyone they'd ever seen.

"Hello? Diane?" I forgot I still had Sandra on the line.

"I'll call you back."

The next thing I remembered, he gave me a piggyback and said he was taking me home. I was not in the state of trusting anyone, not even Jake. I knew that sex was trouble, and Jake was trouble. But why was the energy emanating from Jake and Sandra so invariably strong?

What worried me more was that my identity was at stake. I couldn't trust anyone.

ANOMALY

I woke up to soft touches on my arm. My eyes opened to Jake, propping his head with one hand while the other stroked me gently. I flinched.

"Easy, are you OK?"

It took a while for those eyelashes to soothe me and the dark brown irises to confirm that I was safe. The cold pack on my forehead was warm.

"Did your ex follow you here?"

"Don't worry about her."

I sat up in bed and was glad to see him fully clothed. The alarm clock showed half past seven. He noticed my inability to relax, my coldness, and my growing panic. Had he not invited me to that goddamn gig, none of the shit would have happened, and my desire for him would still be the same. He handed me a glass of water, telling me to hydrate. Had he stayed up and watched me all night? Did he go through any of my stuff? It would have been years since I had someone stay over who knew who I was.

"I really like you, Diane," he said, and things began to blur before me.

"Are you sure your ex didn't follow you here? Are there more exes I need to worry about, Jake?"

"Holy fuck! Chill out!"

It felt like he had prepared something to say, but I ruined the vibe. Frustration was etched on his face, and there was something very human about it that I couldn't connect with.

"I took care of it, OK?" He stopped talking and sighed. Then he got off the bed with the gel pack and walked into the kitchen. I grabbed my phone and saw two missed calls from Sandra and three unread texts. It looked like he'd ignored them. I heard the fridge door open and close. After a moment of silence, I heard his contemplative footsteps on the creaky laminate flooring in the living room.

Standing at my bedroom door now, holding his leather jacket, he looked defeated, an expression I'd never seen on him before. Even though we barely knew each other for a long time, it felt like we'd been dating since the day we met.

"Is Sandra your girlfriend?" he asked.

"What if I said she was? Did you date her, too?"

He scoffed, swinging his jacket over his shoulder, and laughed. "Yes, I did date a Sandra a while back."

"Was she much younger than you and from Leeds?" I said.

He gave a slight grimace of pain, but I couldn't tell whether he knew what I was talking about. Suddenly something dawned on him.

"You remind me of me right now," he said. "When I had my head injury, I was paranoid too. But I had a good reason to be. I woke up to the biggest nightmare of my life. I didn't want the same to happen to you. And if you can't trust me, I understand. But I wanted you to know that it was never easy for me to open up to someone. I finally got it off my chest, and it didn't matter if the world knew. It's like having moved on from something, and now I can focus on helping others…"

He trailed off as if he hadn't planned to say any of that, not in that kind of fashion anyway.

"Please leave, Jake."

He nodded understandingly, his gaze down. His retwisted microlocs were dangling forward. I hadn't noticed his hair was different, not even during the show.

As he turned to leave, he said, "I want you to have your head checked, Diane. And be sure to take your meds, OK?"

When he finally walked out the door, I made sure I locked it and put the bar on. Next, I went back to bed and pulled the duvet over my head.

Jake and I had more in common than I thought. He left his iPod and earphones on the night table beside my pill bottle. I didn't like the fact that he saw it and told me to take it, so I tossed the bottle in the bin.

Strangely enough, he didn't even miss the music he left behind. From Joy Division to Red Hot Chili Peppers and other stuff we both liked, they all defined him so much better than what I saw on stage. I moved to the side of the bed where he had laid and breathed in the faint smell of cedar.

I didn't leave my flat for three days and was thus behind with my next interview and story. I never had my head checked either, assuming enough rest would get me back on my feet. The symptoms of nausea and fatigue had also subsided.

Sandra told me she'd gone to see a spiritualist to work on improving her healing energies and gathering some self-discovery. I had upset her when I questioned her about Jake and the relations she might have had with him. Since the bottle incident, I couldn't help but question everyone I felt close to. But she denied it all and was on the verge of tears when I continued to push her on FaceTime. Her beautiful virgin aura also shone through, and I apologised.

I spent a lot of time reading the local news, and one story stood out to me. It showed a picture of a smiling, blond woman who looked familiar. The fake red leather pants...Her name was Lauren Black. The title said, "Suicide or Murder?" Lauren was found dead at home near Hulme two nights ago. She had hung herself in the bath, using a makeshift rope made of her bedsheet that she'd attached to the shower head and wrapped the other end around her neck. According to the story, her face was painted like a clown, and she was sodomised with a sex toy. Her last call was made to her ex-boyfriend. Police assumed he was involved and he was under investigation. My heart sank. I quickly checked my website and social channels and dug up Jake's story. The news was only posted that morning, yet I worried what it might do to my story.

My mailbox was flooded with emails, and comments under Jake's story quadrupled overnight. Though the press didn't mention Jake's name in the article, the people instantly made the connection, and so did my readers. I skimmed through comments containing the keyword *murderer*. At least one out of twenty-five would refer to Lauren as a lying bitch. A shiver ran down my spine when I moved on to the emails. It didn't take me long to find an email from Lauren dated three nights ago. It would have been after Jake had supposedly dealt with her.

It was a short message saying: "I would have walked through fire for Jake, and still he chose you. But there is one more thing I would do for him. And soon, everyone will know about you."

I didn't understand what it meant, nor could I tell whether my hard-earned photoblog was coming to an end. Then, I was distracted by the preacher outside my building, talking about

Noah's ark. He said that this time around, no one would be embarking on the vessel.

Another day went by and the news didn't continue to pursue Lauren's story, so there were no further mentions of Jake. Luckily, the police never tried to reach me either. The last thing I needed was to come forward and face the public. And for what? Some jealous bitch who clearly killed herself for attention? It bothered me that Jake had become the ultimate anomaly of my photoblog. I thought Joseph was an anomaly after learning his backstory from Sandra. Had Joseph's life been a fictional story, adding the prequel would have been debasing. But a lot of people viewed fiction as a travesty anyway. In Jake's case, I knew too much about his life to view it as a piece of fiction.

When my mum visited and saw the bruise on my forehead, she dragged me to our family doctor to have it checked. In fact, the bruising looked a lot worse than the bump itself. While we were in the waiting room, my mum reminded me to get my medication refill and then mumbled about why I wasn't getting married or seeking a proper job. Nobody understood that all I wanted was to be alone and write. As long as I wasn't indebted or broke, things were good in my eyes. I remained quiet, staring at my phone, reading texts from Sandra telling me she'd been feeding a wild dove that came to see her every day. I told her to name her new pet, but she said no, as she didn't intend to possess it. After saying that, she realised it was time to let go of her ex for good and work on that upward spiral. But I knew she wasn't going to do that.

BUTCHER GIRL

I had no nausea, vomiting, or headache symptoms, so that was enough for my family doctor to say I was good to go. It was a waste of my time, and Jake was right. After all, I didn't fall head-first on linoleum flooring and lose consciousness.

After lunch with my mum, I headed down Mosley Street towards the Central Library. I liked picking a random book and then going up to the reading room on the first floor, which was known as the Great Hall. It had a huge dome-like oculus window on the ceiling that let in natural light. It was a hall of whispers and often a good place to encounter an interesting story. I just needed one breath of words that made me pick that particular person.

When taking a seat in one of the study carrels, I put on my face mask and beanie and opened the book that I randomly picked from the Russian literature section. There was barely any author I hadn't read.

And it happened to be Dostoevsky's *House of the Dead*, which I had never bothered to finish. Even though I was a sucker for semi-autobiographical fiction, that book was too loosely-knit, so it failed to hold my attention. I never finished it and didn't intend to do it that day. Strangely enough, the protagonist was sentenced to prison in Siberia for ten years after murdering his wife. The picture of a dead girl wearing a clown face came to mind, although a picture of Lauren's last breath was never published.

And suddenly, the whispers in the room became more audible, even five desks down. I leaned my head against the left divider and entered a dream-like state. A woman was on the phone with her boyfriend, whispering. But she was unaware that I was able to hear every single word and frustrated tone that came from her breath.

"I'm sorry for what you're going through," she said. "But I can't do this anymore. I just can't."

I imagined what the boyfriend was saying to her. Perhaps something along the lines of, "But we still love each other. That's when you stick together and work things out, right?"

She said with a sob, "I don't think so. I don't feel that way anymore…"

When she hung up, I stood up, ready to approach her for the interview of her life. But I suddenly felt someone looking at me from the other side of the line of carrels. Even from my peripherals, I knew him from somewhere, but I couldn't place him anywhere then.

I walked over to the girl, a petite brunette, and sat on the chair next to her. She had big brown chestnut eyes similar to Sandra's, except this lady seemed more mature and serious. It could be the stress wrinkles, the thin lines of crow's feet. She was startled by me and, at the same time, embarrassed.

"Come with me," I said and removed my face mask. "I promise you that everything will be OK."

When I held out my hand to her, she hesitated at first. Again, from my peripherals, I saw the familiar figure stand up and gaze at us. She grabbed my hand, and we both walked out of the hall. It felt like we were both running away from something, and it felt good, as though we had each other's back.

As she was still drying her eyes, I said, "I'm going to take you to the library café where I'll buy you a coffee. We'll chat about our favourite books, the arseholes we dated, and the better days that are yet to come. But today is all about you, hun."

There was no reason for a stranger to trust me when I approached them, especially when they were in their most vulnerable state. But when I wanted something so bad, I would think of the most bullshit thing to say. I was no longer OK with "no" for an answer. The strange thing was that I never used to be that way.

When I interviewed Susan that afternoon, she had all my attention; she was my safe place for almost seventy minutes, as though I was watching one of my favourite movies or was high on a drug for a moment. Despite being quite the crybaby, she was quick to regain her composure. Surprisingly, she didn't mention her boyfriend once, as he had never been the primary issue in her life. She had a dark past to unearth—one that had hindered everyone from understanding who she was. Life had sucked out all of her energy reserves, leading to an excessive need for self-care. Her biggest fear was becoming a mother. Despite caring so deeply, she couldn't see herself taking care of anyone or anything. At the end of the interview, she smiled for the first time. She got rid of that heavy load in merely seventy minutes, whereas other troubled people would waste over a thousand quid on therapy or jeopardise friendships by unloading on their friends.

After taking a photograph of Susan and signing some paperwork, we hugged each other goodbye. All that time, I'd felt eyes on us, but I no longer cared. When leaving the Central Library, I had the urge to see my father at work. Since I knew my mother had errands to run and wouldn't be there, I went to see him.

When I entered the shop, my dad didn't even need to look up to know it was me.

"Daughter," he said.

"Father."

The flatscreen TV was showing the news about the River Mersey flooding. It had already washed out the coast of Liverpool, and the tide was now making its way inland. People in the town of Warrington were getting ready to evacuate. It seemed their £30 million flood defence scheme wasn't good enough.

Dad was preparing cuts of meat that looked like beef sirloin. He was good at preparing meat displays in neat order. Daily sale items would be immediately visible as one walked in to get dinner ideas. That day, he had lamb chops on sale for twenty-five per cent off. I didn't go in there often because my dad didn't like me there. After all, there had almost been a murder because of me.

"What brings you here? Shouldn't you be looking for a job?"

"Just getting some frozen beef bones. And I told you I was freelancing."

He nodded at the deep freezers at the back of the shop and said, "Where is the job security in freelancing?"

His thick Chinese accent bothered me, but I'd rather not speak in our own language. He would only speak English with me when he wanted to keep up with the conversation and have my attention.

"Your mother said you ran against a glass door and broke it. But I don't think your head is hard enough to break glass."

I remained quiet and thought about how glass didn't always break when it hit the ground. Lying to your parents may be the dumbest thing you can do, but it's also the best way to say you don't want to talk about something.

"I guess not."

"We're just worried about you," he said.

"I know."

"We believe you have what it takes to be a good journalist…or writer, whatever. You just need to try harder."

I walked up to the counter with the bag of beef bones for which I wanted to pay. That was when I realised he had been watching me for a while—the most attention I ever got within a few minutes' time.

"Leave the past in the past," he said dryly. "Let it go."

"Did Buddha say that?"

A customer walked in, and he told me to get out before he could answer my question. His voice and facial expression changed instantly as he greeted a big ginger lady whom I recognised as one of the regular customers.

He hadn't cashed in the ten quid I left on the counter, but he would notice sooner or later.

"Love you, Dad."

He didn't hear it, but the fat lady did. She ignored it and resumed the small talk that my dad had initiated.

Sandra sent me a long email the next morning, but it didn't read like it was addressed to me. It was addressed to her ex, marking the day of their one-year anniversary. That explained why she was getting drunk on her own the past few nights. She would send me links to music by Elliot Smith and Bon Ivor, none of which interested me at all. When she was like that, I felt it was important to keep her talking, focusing on a conversation with me about the fun we had in Reykjavik. But it was difficult to keep her focused on the phone when she was drunk, as she would slur for a second about the past and then talk euphorically about what a wonderful, mindful person I was and how much she loved me. She wanted me to understand what my Venus square Pluto meant and see how intense my love was and how transformative it was to my lovers. During that, she brought up Jake and said she'd changed her mind about him because she found it romantic how he'd carried me home and said the things he said.

But there was something very unsettling in that email, especially when I took the time to capture the details of how she was never going to be over that person. After all, he had hindered her from killing herself that year I met her. I had to take breaks from that email as it was so intense and filled with love for someone who was clearly not worthy of it, and that included myself. I skipped to the screenshots she attached, which were text message conversations between her and her ex. She had blurred out his name whenever she addressed him. On each and every line, she was offering pure love to him, reminding him of how he had saved her.

Close to the end of the email, I held my breath. There was a name. She wanted me to know. I suddenly remembered who I saw at the library, the person watching me when I approached Susan.

INTREPID URBAN FOX

I didn't understand Sandra's intent for sending me the email, nor was I sure she was either. For all I knew, she could have been an informant. I did not reply, and we never spoke of it. She called me the next day, acting as if she'd never sent me anything.

"Have you talked to Jake?" she asked.

"No. Why?"

"Don't you want to know if he's OK?"

"You seem more concerned than me."

She scoffed, and I knew she'd been keeping an eye on the news like me. I wanted to change the subject by bringing up her email, but I didn't. She was already vulnerable. She switched the call to FaceTime, and the first thing she commented on was my bruise. She looked youthful and beautiful as ever with her lively curls and glowing eyes, but the half curve on the corner of her mouth suggested a deep, painful secret.

"Do you think Jake had something to do with that girl's death?"

"No," I said. She was careful when choosing her words—not mentioning murder or suicide.

"How are you so sure?"

My fingers were playing with Jake's earphones, and a sudden chill ran down my spine when an email popped up just above Sandra's forehead, so I swiped it away.

"Because Lauren emailed me before she died, saying she'd do anything for him. And she vowed to dox me."

"Wow. Is that legal?" she said.

"She's dead. Who gives a fuck?"

Sandra went pale for a moment, but instead of asking what her theory was, I had my own. For all I knew, it was the same as hers, but I just couldn't share it with her.

"What information would she have about you, though?"

"Enough?"

"Is there something you're not telling me, Diane?"

I shrugged at my phone, not looking at her, as I must have turned white myself. I thought about the home I wrecked over a year ago, except that his partner never confronted me about it face-to-face. Knowing life well enough, the past always had a bone to pick with you. I changed the subject.

"I interviewed someone the other day. She just wanted to live her life according to her own rules. No compromises. No restrictions. No delays. I told her she'd be a successful woman one day."

"It's so odd how you connect with these strangers," Sandra said.

"Why?"

"I think it's the little things that count. All you want is the big meal, and once you've digested it, you're over it."

"That's not true!"

She rolled her eyes. She didn't understand why I wouldn't stay *friends* with my interviewees.

"That's not how it works with my subjects," I said.

"You call them *subjects*?"

"Yes, why?"

"That's such a psychopathic thing to say, Diane!"

I didn't know what she meant. People want to be heard; people want to be in the spotlight, and all I did was pick the most impactful voices. She couldn't expect me to be *friends* with hundreds of people I met for a mere sixty- to ninety-minute interview. It wasn't like they gave a shit about me. And approaching them anonymously was the only way to obtain authenticity with no bias. Why didn't anybody get it? There were never ever going to be any "little things."

The email came from Adam, the host of the Intrepid Urban Fox podcast. Before I read it, I went straight to the attachment. Someone took a photograph of Jake and me at the Arch Bridge. The person must have been close without us realising it because it showed my clear face under the street lights, and Jake was sneakily grinning at me. Adam wrote:

I received this from Lauren Black. And then I saw you. I know you saw me too. Please, can we meet? - Adam.

What was he going to do, blackmail me? What was his relation to Lauren? Instead of speculating, I texted him to meet me at the Central Library right away. He replied that he'd be there in five minutes, whereas I had a longer way to walk. Five minutes later, he texted, asking how I liked my coffee, but it just infuriated me more.

"Black it is…" he wrote.

I climbed the concrete stairs with heavy steps and headed towards the café. Instantly I spotted the British version of Mark Hoppus, seated in the corner with his back facing the public.

"I want to sit in this chair, please."

I startled him, and he almost spilt his coffee. He didn't even look at me as he said, "People are more likely to recognise me than *you*, Diane."

He slowly gazed at me and smiled that cocky smile of his. He looked exactly like he did on his podcast—expressive and charismatic, which I hated to admit. Then, he lowered his gaze and pointed at the chair across from him or the coffee he got for me.

"It smells like a medium roast, I only drink dark."

"Nice to meet you, too," he said.

I slowly moved to the other chair, pulling my beanie further down my forehead to cover my bruise properly. After being blue the day before, it had turned purple-yellow when I met Adam. After I finally sat down, I noticed a proud smirk at the corners of his mouth. How did I not notice the tingle I'd felt the first time he greeted me on video? And how could I not tell that his eyes were gunmetal blue? What the fuck did he want from me?

When I heard a Stereophonics song playing in the background, goosebumps rose on my forearms, and I pulled my black sleeves down.

"Are you OK? You seem tensed up, Diane."

It was hot. I lowered my head and pulled my beanie all the way down to cover my face. The sound of my hair going static had me freeze for a moment. When I uncovered my face without adjusting my messy hair, Adam said, "Holy shit. What happened to you?"

"Your groupie of an informant did that."

"Oh, wow," he said. "Listen, I don't know who she was. I'd never seen her in my life until the news and the email."

I leaned forward and placed the lukewarm coffee aside. "What do you want from me, Adam? Money? I don't have any. Exposure? Well, I think that bitch already screwed me over."

He scoffed and then gave off a painful laugh. "I'm sorry if that's what you think of me, really."

He leaned back and actually looked hurt when he pinched at a loose seam on his navy blue shirt. Did he have an ulterior motive, or was he actually acting genuinely?

I wondered what Sandra saw in him because I remember reading how intelligent she thought he was and how his Aquarian energies were so original, honest, and logical. All I saw was guardedness, hidden despair, and something else I couldn't quite fathom. Sandra trusted her instincts more than I did, in a way I would deem naive or impulsive. She and I had a deep connection, but how deep would her love be in a relationship with someone? Suffocatingly deep.

"The truth is," he said, "I was just very intrigued and curious about you. I don't have a motive. Trust me or not. But I sincerely like your photoblog—I never would want to do anything to jeopardise what you created. Building something from nothing takes time and a little bit of luck. I've been there and know how much consistent hard work it takes."

He finished the last sip of his coffee and pushed back his chair a tad. I laid my hand on his and felt a sudden warmth rushing through my fingertips.

"I'm sorry," I said, and it was all I could say without expanding into something pathetic created from self-pity. When I saw a half smile, I removed my hand instantly.

"You're not how I imagined you, Diane, and believe me, it's a good thing."

People had compared me to an Asian version of Lisbeth Salander, but more subtle. I saw no similarity because she was ten times stronger and actually cared.

I put on my beanie and adjusted it in a way that would cover my bruise again. The Stereophonics song ended. Adam moved the chair closer to the table again. More heat emanated from his body, and I couldn't help but succumb to that tingling feeling in my chest.

"Would you like a fresh dark roast," he said.

I shook my head.

After an awkward silence, he smiled. "Do you remember when I asked you whether you would have picked me as an interviewee had you seen me at the library?"

I nodded.

"Suppose I got my answer," he said. "But there is nothing wrong with being selective. I am the same."

His face flushed for a second as though embarrassed about oversharing.

"But enough about me. Can I ask you something?"

I shrugged.

"Why do you do what you do?"

I said, "Self-preservation, I guess. Finding myself in others maintains my belief in humanity. It's just a shame this connection never lasts."

"It's because you're after the big meal."

Why was everyone thinking about food?

"All the little things or little bites," he said, "are for those who think they have the time to spare. They believe that little meaningful things add to the big picture, which—they do eventually—the longer they believe in it. But this is not the type of sustainability everybody wants. You really don't want to fool yourself."

Who is *you*? I suddenly remembered what it was about him that intimidated me—the belief that human existence contained no value, his extreme scepticism towards meaning, or the attempt to create it. He was all about laying everything bare on the table. How could I tell him that it wasn't how things worked for me?

I leaned forward and said, "I would fuck Camus back to life if I could. And I get that his philosophy is for hopeless, infatuated brats like me. But if I hadn't been fooling myself, I would've put myself in an early grave. What makes you so different? Or let me ask you the same question: Why do *you* do what you do, Adam?"

Before he had a chance to say anything, I continued, "Let me guess, you want to pass the time; you want to be heard; you want to—connect. But people are like drugs to you; the high wears off, and you move on, not giving a shit about the damage you caused and left behind."

Something lit up in his eyes, and I was certain we were thinking about the same girl with big brown eyes. I hoped he didn't suspect me of knowing something.

"There is no point for appetisers, is there, Diane?" he said. "Whether you're a fool or not, you're certainly not a blind one."

I leaned back in my chair, succumbing to the increased heart rate. I overshared. He and I sought the same kind of high, and that was where our mutual flaw lay. But who could resent us?

"Do you know which one of your stories enticed me the most?" he said. "It's the one with the session player who almost got murdered."

I looked at him, trying to remain calm and disinterested, but he made sure I had his full attention.

He continued, "Now you interview another musician, and an actual death occurred. What are the odds?"

His eyes became sombre. He already knew the truth but wanted to hear it from me.

"What are you not telling me, Adam?"

If only I could wipe off that cocky grin from that faraway horizon. Each time I felt I was close to something, he revealed a new trigger that had me believe he was on to me. If I were ever to trust those gunmetal blue eyes, I could get shot in the back. No matter what his intentions were, he had already entered my realm.

"These people are using me as their V-weapon, Diane."

"People?"

"Lauren Black lost her mind when you shagged her ex, but who gives a shit? The story of Chris Taylor, on the other hand, is far more intriguing."

"Why is that?"

He tapped his fingers on the table, wondering if I knew what was coming. "Because it's about you."

"Don't be daft," I said.

Adam hesitated, acting like he was about to break a sacred deal he'd closed with someone. He turned away for two seconds and then looked at me sharply, saying, "His partner Greg Ferrell reached out to me and told me how he made you tell that story instead of Chris's original story."

Of course, he did.

Yes. Chris, the session player, had told me a much more intriguing story, which I should have shared instead. Lies weren't worth a thing, not even on the brink of death, but Greg made me do it. After Greg's edits, the girl involved in the story deserved to die even more.

As the sight of Adam turned blurry, I closed my eyes. I wasn't surprised that Jake's story, plus the news about Lauren Black, had stirred something up in Greg. He probably believed that I killed Lauren with my bare hands and that I was playing with the emotionally unstable.

"You see, the perspective in Chris's story is off. It lacks a certain genuineness. I actually don't believe the ending," he said.

I scoffed deliriously at his comment but didn't grant him a "Bravo, you read between the lines." What was the point? My whole fucking empire was a joke. If he didn't burn me at the stake, somebody else would. My dad had always known that I was a millennial fuckup.

Suddenly I was the one who couldn't stop grinning. While doing so, Adam looked slightly confused, but that just made him more handsome. He conjured up a memory I'd had trouble facing for a long time. But I was no longer afraid of the past. I rose from my seat and leaned forward across the table to study Adam's facial features. Stacking my elbows on the table and propping my chin in my palms, I closely examined the pores on the sides of his nose. He had a light scruff look—long stubble that covered his philtrum and chin. I could tell he was my age. His gaze rested on my lip ring for a long time before our eyes locked.

"Let me guess," I said, "Greg wants you to reveal my identity to the public and link Chris's story to the result of my publishing Jake's story."

Adam had made many controversial moves by debunking myths, stories, beliefs, and much more on his podcast. So why wouldn't he debunk a person? His online presence depicted the ideal playground to strip me of my reputation and put an end to my photoblog. But it wasn't what he wanted.

"Unless," I said.

"You share Chris's original story with me."

And there was the motive.

I heard a ringing in my ear, and my sense of balance shook me in the form of a hypnagogic jerk like I was falling asleep.

"Are you OK?" he asked. "You fell asleep for a microsecond."

My knee began to shake when I pictured beautiful Chris in the butcher shop with me. Then my phone vibrated several times in my front pocket, but I ignored it.

Adam was analysing my every move now, knowing very well that I was not drunk or on coke. I leaned back, opened the small zipper of my sleeve pocket and pulled out a tiny USB stick that was half the size of my thumb.

"We can eat some popcorn and listen to it if you like," I said. "But just to warn you in advance, that story is cursed, and someone might die."

He thought I was flirting, but I wasn't.

"You know what?" he said. "I'm not much of an audio guy. I prefer the way you put it down into written words."

"Oh, well—same thing."

"No," he said. "People might not see it, but it's you who breathes life into their stories. You filter out all the bullshit. I couldn't give a shit about your subjects unless their stories are filtered through you."

Did he just call them *subjects*, too? I was speechless. It was something brand-new to me and not really fathomable. It reminded me of something Sandra said. She said I had a large capacity for dark things and that, at times, I made my subjects' stories appear darker than they really were.

"I'm sorry, it sounds weird, Diane," he said. "Whether you share it with me or not, I have no intention of dropping the bomb. Besides, I choose who and what I want to debunk. I might be a prick at times, but I'm not a weapon or tool for other people's retaliation projects."

DISAPPEARING COMPLETELY

I asked Adam to take me home to his place, which was only three blocks away from the Central Library. I wore my mask and sunglasses in case Lauren Black had a twin with a camera stalking us. It was difficult to breathe in the late afternoon heat. My floating mind was in control of my body, and I simply let the impulses drive me to whatever edge I might be reaching. Adam was tall—six foot something. The ground on which he and I were walking didn't feel solid. The Mancunian noise of nearby trams heading towards Deansgate or Oxford Road, skater kids practising their ollies on concrete, corporate people gossiping about their superiors, climate change protesters—all that proved that I was still present. Or was I not? I touched the zipper on my sleeve to make sure I'd put the USB back in there, and the last thing I remember was grabbing Adam's arm when I lost track of the ground.

I stepped into a creek with my leather boots, but as I looked ahead of me, I realised it was a fast-flowing river, funnelling towards what looked like a plunge waterfall. The stream picked up its pace, and I was pushed by the strong current towards the fall. Though I never learned how to swim front crawl, I knew how to do it in my dream. I just wasn't fast enough. And before the shore got out of reach, I saw something forming in the sand. I recognised Jake's figure rising and reaching out a hand. His entire body was golden and grainy—those broad shoulders still greatly emphasised, and his muscular legs, like tree trunks, were planted to the ground. As I continued swimming towards him, I gasped for air and swallowed a lot of water on the way. The truth was I couldn't swim front crawl but only believed that I could. When Jake saw the water dragging me further away from him, he did something else with his hands. He stretched out his fingers, pointing at the water and began absorbing it through his fingertips. I didn't know that sand grains' tiny pores could hold so much water. Just like that, it was all gone.

With my right cheek pressing hard against the wet soil, my ear perceived the sound of small steps approaching. I coughed up some excess water. Underneath the light weight of the person's feet, I heard how they pressed against the water beneath the surface—the gritty sound of grains as dry sand gets caught between the toes.

"Your Black Moon Lilith is in Pisces," the voice said.

I gazed up at Sandra's partly silhouetted face. She continued, "I told you there is a lot of water."

"What does it mean, Sandra?"

"That you're a self-destructive wreck. Fucking drown already."

I woke up with a dry throat and a light headache. I was lying on a couch; the room smelled like stale cigarette smoke. Gazing over to the table, there was an ashtray, several piles of books, cigarette paper, and crumpled notebook pages.

"Good, you're awake," said Adam as he walked into the room with a glass of water with ice. "You really need to hydrate."

As I sat up and grabbed my upper arm, I realised he'd removed my hoodie with the sleeve zipper.

"Where is my hoodie?"

He placed the glass in front of me and walked over to his desk chair—my hoodie was on the armrest.

When he tossed it at me, he said, "You were sweating really bad."

Adam didn't look at me and appeared very casual. My phone fell out onto my lap, showing two missed calls and three unread text messages from Sandra. Without reading them, I stuffed the phone back into the pocket and touched the sleeve zipper to make sure my USB was there.

"How long was I out for?"

"Not long, about ten minutes," he said. "I almost took you to the emergency."

He had disappeared into the kitchen by then and shouted, "Are you hungry? Do you want a proper drink? Or a paracetamol?"

I looked at his desk, which was just as messy as the coffee table, if not worse, with a couple of wine glasses, unopened letters, and other rubbish. Still, his one-bedroom flat bore a similar resemblance to mine, minus the cigarettes and booze. He had the same wallpaper on his iMac as me—the Big Sur Road.

"No," I said. "But you may need a proper drink."

He laughed somewhat nervously, probably unaware of what was coming next. He mumbled something I didn't hear because he was pulling a cork out of a wine bottle.

The windows were open, and the smell of petrichor hit my nostrils, conjuring up a moment far away from here. The setting was familiar and precognitive, revealing a sense of nostalgia to which I was unable to succumb because the picture of Chris flashed before me, longing to be set free. I drank the whole glass of water and chewed on a piece of ice. It just started to rain. The room was hot and humid. When the cold water flushed through my system, I felt an instant pain in my oesophagus.

"Are you sure you don't want anything?"

"More ice," I said, feeling a sense of compulsion that I could not suppress.

By the time Adam entered the living room with a wine bottle and a glass of ice cubes, he found me naked on his couch. He would soon understand why it was important since he'd asked for it.

In my hand, I held pieces of paper that had been folded five times. They were old and badly crinkled at the edges.

Adam didn't move or blink for a while—not until I placed my feet down and unclipped my lip ring. After tossing it into the ashtray, I looked at him in dead earnest. When people say that history repeats itself, they are referring to themselves.

"Filtered through me, right?"

I knew he didn't want to read it on his computer, nor did he want to listen to the original voice recording. He wanted me to read the original interview out loud. I had a sudden longing for Chris, and while I was already there, I, too, wanted a piece of the cake. Even if it was just one more bite. This shouldn't be happening, but no past ever remains buried, not if you have lied about it.

As I spoke Chris's words, Adam had almost turned into stone. He didn't light his cigarette or pour himself the wine he'd opened. He was sitting in his chair across from me, leaning forward with his elbows resting on his knees and hands clasped.

"So it really was about you," Adam said, looking down. "You were lovers before you even did the interview."

I put my bra, shirt and panties back on and regretted having tossed my lip ring into the ashtray. Adam studied every move as though wondering whether I was wearing organic cotton or he was imagining me in silk.

"Yeah, and I swore to myself not to do it again. This was the most biased story and interview I ever did. And that's when you get destructive outcomes like this."

"So you fucked Jake after the interview?"

"Why are you so interested in my sex life, Adam?" I said.

"You're so careful with whom you choose. And no matter whom you choose, there's trouble. But it seems that you, too, have a taste for disaster. It gives you a fucking kick. Admit it."

That grin was back. It suddenly felt like a test or a challenge. I knew I would rouse something in him, but I hadn't thought further.

My phone buzzed inside my hoodie, but we both ignored it. A few seconds later, his phone on the desk buzzed too.

"I should get going," I said as I stood up and tried to walk past him.

He remained seated, raising an arm to block my way. Without looking at me, he bit his lower lip. "It's still pissing out."

"Where's the loo?" I said.

Awkwardly, he lowered his arm and gestured at the hallway. "To the left."

I heard him take a deep breath as I headed that way. I locked the door behind me and peed for almost a whole minute. The bathroom was unusually clean for a single bloke, unlike the living area. Clean subway tiles in the shower with neat grout lines and a quartz countertop and backsplash. I didn't check the toilet before I sat on it, but I knew it was clean also. It was almost like he never used anything in here, or he'd hired a crime scene cleaner.

Sandra had spammed my phone. Starting from the top of the message feed, she first apologised for calling me "psychopathic" and then said she needed to talk to me, it was regarding an email she'd sent. Next, she said it was urgent and begged me not to ignore her. I texted that I'd call her later. Right away, she attempted to call again, but I was washing my hands and didn't want to answer.

When I opened the door, Adam stood right there, a whole head taller than me. He cupped my cheeks tightly with his large hands and kissed me. While he pressed against my body with all his weight, I fell seated on the toilet lid with my back leaning against the porcelain tank. The tank lid rattled, the seat shifted, and I tasted wine.

I threw my arms around his neck and wrapped my legs around his torso when he lifted me up and grabbed me by the buttocks. He carried me out of the bathroom and down the hallway, but before he granted me access to his bedroom, he slammed my body against the wall. The back of my head hit the thin drywall, but it didn't hurt as much as he'd intended. I felt his erection through his black jeans and how much it was hurting him.

Next, I felt his right hand grip around my neck, and he warned me, "So that you know, I've been honest with you all the way. No tricks, no lies. Can I expect the same from you?"

"No," I gasped.

"Why, you just made it all the more interesting."

His breath was hot and sweet, his gunmetal blue eyes had turned black. As I continued gasping, I saw Jake's face—the night we first made love. Were I to die in that instant, it would be in a kiss because I would drag the person along with me. I pressed Adam's head against mine before I disappeared completely.

ONE EYE OPEN

It always cooled down so quickly after the rain, and surprisingly, the clouds had cleared fast, too. I felt strangely secure and at ease, which I hadn't in a long time. It wouldn't take long for guilt to seep through, though.

With Adam's bedroom facing the east, I couldn't see the sunset. I would have to stay the night to see it rise in the morning. I was lying on the edge of his bed, belly down, my right cheek pressed into the pillow. The other half of my face gazed at the blue sky. All I smelled was cigarette smoke coming from the other room. It made no difference whether he smoked in his own bedroom or not.

Sandra stopped trying to call an hour ago. I had turned the vibration off and placed my phone on the floor, face down.

Adam was on the phone in the living room, talking quietly, but I could hear every single word:

"What do you want me to do about it? I thought we were clear on this…No, I did not…Why should I? The answer is no."

He talked to a girl, and I knew everything she was saying; I even knew how she felt deep down. His voice was firm, and his reserved nature showed no sign of annoyance or anger. If I were to interpret what he said and his tone, I would almost think he cared.

I heard him enter the room and sit on the bed. There was a minute of silence before he decided to climb all the way in and lean against the headboard.

"I'm not sure if you're aware," he said, "but you bled all over my bed."

"Sorry. The neck of my womb gets sensitive sometimes."

He scoffed. "How did it not hurt? Do you even feel anything?"

It wasn't a funny joke, but I laughed at it almost deliriously.

"Never mind the bruise on your forehead, but the one on your left thigh looks way worse," he said, hoping I would elaborate on it, but I didn't.

"I can't really fathom who you are, Diane. But you sure know how to keep things intriguing."

I thought of a quote from a movie I couldn't remember, but it was a character played by Michael Caine. He said you could have all the accomplishments in the world and still not be able to fathom your own heart. How was that for motivation? Perhaps my heart was still thawing like the glacier on Pluto. It was what Sandra believed. I was honestly more concerned about the potential flood it could cause.

"I'll replace your sheets."

He laughed and rolled over to spoon me. "I love you, butcher girl," he said, and it sounded like another joke. "You can bleed on whatever you like."

I rolled over to face him and noticed that something had changed in his smile. He wasn't joking.

"Can I ask you something?" he said. "What was on your mind when Chris held the knife over you?"

I returned to facing the window where a plane was flying past, drawing white lines of smoke. In reality, those were vapour trails that turned into ice crystals. I would have felt a chill if Adam hadn't been holding me. There was the guilt.

"Nothing was on my mind," I said. "I took what I believed was my last breath and closed my eyes. I listened to his mild sobs and how he shakingly breathed through his teeth."

"And before that, you told him he had to kill you first."

Yes, I had threatened to tell Greg every detail otherwise, but Greg would have found out either way. The goal was to win some time so the police would turn up in time before anything would happen. But then Chris decided that Greg deserved to know the truth and slit his own throat on top of me.

He survived, though. How else would he have retold the story? And publishing Greg's version of the story was one of the most painful experiences in my life.

"What about you, Adam? Do you think suicide is justifiable?"

He released me and leaned back against the headboard.

"Was it so wrong of me to try to stop Chris from doing it?" I said.

After a long pause, he said, "No. Although you did it for selfish reasons…"

As he talked, I grabbed my phone, tapped voice memo, and hit record before I silently laid it back on the floor.

He continued, "When someone is suicidal, and you grow fond of them, you will know that they have already derailed because…they met you."

When I turned to face him, he didn't look back at me; instead, his mind was completely elsewhere.

"You convince them to stick around for longer just to break them a little more. And to your surprise, they even enjoy it. They think you're the best thing that has ever happened to them. But in the end, they're in a worse place than they were before. And that's when you drop them because you know you can't save them, nor did you ever plan to do that. You were nothing but a little distraction."

He finally looked at me, and again, we were thinking about the same person. His lips looked dry. I think he craved a cigarette.

He continued, "At the café, you said that I treated people like drugs and that I didn't care about the damage I caused. But the damage was already done before I laid my hands on them. All I did was add some colour. It gets a smile or two out of them. That must be worth something, right?"

He showed me another genuine smile, which had something haunting about it. It even carried a little load of sadness. He reached inside his jeans pocket and pulled out my lip ring, placing it on the sheet in front of me.

"What if they fell in love with you?" I said. "If they believed that you healed them?"

"That's when you realise you broke them. Because all of a sudden, they try to fix you. And that's when you'll see a side of me you'd never want to know."

I now realised that his eyes were still black; the smile was long gone. He emanated something dark that was eerily familiar and reminded me of what others had said about me. I understood now what Sandra saw in him and what her intentions were. But I also feared for her, knowing exactly what was coming.

"If they think I healed them, they're delusional. But it doesn't mean I don't love them."

-

At around four in the morning, I opened my eyes wide. The door squeaked, and I turned to see a streak of curly hair vanish. The living room appeared to be lit, but Adam was asleep next to me. My body shook terribly as I got out of bed. I couldn't remember the last time I took my pills, and I had the urge to swallow something— something white or something colourful. The torch on my phone was playing up. When it finally illuminated the floor, I tip-toed out of the room.

Adam's desk lamp was on, and so was his iMac screen, showing his Google Mail inbox. Next to the keyboard was a new pack of paracetamol he'd just opened. I swallowed one before I sat down in front of the monitor and scanned the list of emails.

Lauren's email was in the middle and sent on the same day as when she reached out to me just a few minutes before. Including the photo attachment, the mail simply said, "Take this bitch down." She was such a cliché, and so was her goddamn suicide.

It felt like my heart skipped a beat when my gaze wandered to Jake in the photograph. Lauren was probably more jealous of her own masterpiece of a shot than me. The 500 mg pill was stuck in my oesophagus, so I gulped down the last sip of his stale wine straight from the open bottle. The screen of my phone illuminated, showing a message from Jake. All it said was, "I need to see you."

I moved the mouse to Greg's email and saw an exhaustingly long page of text. It included details Adam had concealed from me. Apparently, Chris had attempted another suicide and was now in a mental institution where he was abused. Only in the spring did I read about a mental health facility scandal about staff allegedly abusing patients. Chris must have been one of those patients. Greg wrote that I was a psycho when I skipped my meds, and so was Chris. And I'd ruined their lives and would only ruin more if Adam didn't call me on it. Adam only replied, asking for the original story without making it sound like some sort of a deal, but Greg refused. Only yesterday afternoon, he wrote to Adam saying that Chris had died. There was no detail on the cause of death or whether it was a suicide.

The email ended with, "You're no different from her. And your pod contributes to nothing."

There were also a bunch of emails from Sandra I didn't bother reading, as I already knew her nature. When I finally opened all her text messages on my phone, I held my breath. Each text was sent with a two- or three-hour gap, describing the different stages she was in. After dressing myself, I made sure I didn't leave anything behind and even peeked into Adam's bedroom. He had not moved, but something told me he was awake and listening to every footstep and keystroke.

Cross Street was quiet. The faint smell of morning dew was evident whenever I wasn't walking past red-brick and concrete buildings. I'd lost interest in those classical gothic structures when they started adding glass buildings in between or on top of them, believing that they signified advanced technology. Why the modern era had to be highlighted in such a fashion was beyond my grasp. Still, it wasn't as bad as London yet, and London was no more.

Victoria Station had also turned into a glass building when they started building around it and added the Metrolink. Everything became so clear at five in the morning—things I was aware of yet never really perceived in a way that affected me personally, like the sunrise reflecting hazily on the Printworks building.

By the time I reached Victoria, the smell of fresh coffee and diesel exhaust struck my nose. A sudden sense of anxiety engulfed me, my heart rate increased, and I hyperventilated. Faraway voices became audible and pierced through my head so intensely that I fell seated on a bench, pressing my ears shut. That was the real Mancunian noise and nothing else. And of all people, I should know it best. If the paracetamol had kicked in, it surely wasn't numbing any pain. Tears were running down my cheeks, and I didn't realise that my sobs were just as loud as the arriving train on platform seven.

With shivering hands, I dialled Jake's number and attempted to maintain my composure. He picked up immediately and said my name with such confidence and determination that I couldn't utter a word.

"Where are you?"

"Jake…"

An announcement came on, and I still had to buy a ticket before hopping on that train to Leeds.

"Are you at the train station? Which one? I'll come get you!"

"Jake, listen to me," I said. "You're the only thing I did right. And you're the only good thing left. Please stay that way."

"I don't understand."

After wiping the snot off my nose, I sniffed and said, "You don't know me."

"I know more than you think. Trust me, Diane. You're not in the right frame of mind…"

Sandra's dad answered the door, which I didn't expect, so I wasn't prepared. Perhaps the surprise visit wasn't a good idea after all.

"Who are you?" he said.

"Hi, I'm Diane. Is Sandra there?"

Mr Williams tried to hide his annoyance but rolled his eyes a little too soon when he heard my name as if I was the corrupt friend from school. Sandra had her dad's facial features, especially the jawline and the shape of the mouth. He had a full lower lip and a thin upper lip that appeared hidden underneath his fine moustache. Her dad's full, wavy, grey hair was the exact copy of Richard Gere's hairstyle in Primal Fear. He was probably in his mid-fifties and struck me as an artist.

"I told her not to talk to you anymore," he said, trying hard to remain polite.

She was in her early twenties, and he still treated her like a teenager.

"And I respect that. I've not been a good friend, and there's so much better she deserves. Please, can I at least tell her that in person? I swear you won't see me here again."

He wanted me gone so bad, but at least he didn't hate me as much as I thought. He jotted something down on paper and passed it to me disapprovingly.

"She was just going to sleep when we left."

His wife called him, asking who was at the door. He said it was nobody and shut the door in my face. The note said Waterloo Manor Hospital. The clinic was six miles outside the city, and I had no clue how to get there on foot or via public transport. Downloading the Uber app would take too long, so I hopped in the next taxi that I saw.

THE END OF HEARTACHE

The clinic was the size of a small, square hotel, painted mustard-yellow and looked like it could be a fancy block of flats. The sun was hot in this part of York, and all I saw on Selby Road were seniors taking walks, either walking their little bichons or Nordic walking proudly to their destination.

I had to see Sandra quickly, but the receptionist was hesitant, telling me that her parents had already visited and she shouldn't be seeing too many people as it could be very overwhelming for her. I said I came all the way from Manchester for the day. The lady said she'd check with Sandra directly and asked me to wait.

In that instant, Adam called, and I stepped outside.

"I hope you found what you were looking for, Diane."

"And what is that?"

"Nothing that I haven't told you. And never mind the little details. They're not important. Of all people, I thought you knew that."

"How were the *little* details about Chris not important to me?"

"Because he's not a part of your life anymore! Don't act like you give a shit!"

I fisted my thigh three times and almost tossed the phone away. I swallowed that scream and said, "This is not your story, Adam!"

He raised his voice, "Then why are you tampering with *mine*?"

He had me stumped, not because it was probably the angriest I'd ever heard him, but because he knew something.

"Do you think I'm stupid?" he said. "I knew you were besties with Sandra—she tells me everything. I suppose that makes me her best friend, not you. Besides, you know shit about us."

It felt like such a ridiculous argument you would have at school with classmates.

"So she's a trivial little detail not worth mentioning to me..."

"You got the drill, butcher girl," he said. "But my interest in you had nothing to do with her. I reached out to you because I genuinely liked your blog. After speaking with you on the pod, you stuck with me. Next, your name started popping up all over the place because of the mess that you created. And then I found out that she'd reached out to you, too."

The sun was bright at eight in the morning, and it felt like the day was already halfway over. How I couldn't wait for it to be over. Too many new stories started to evolve, and I was barely done dealing with the old ones. As a mild breeze brushed against my face, I scoffed at the sun and laughed with my eyes squinting.

"What?" he said.

I didn't realise I was still on the phone with him and tried to collect my thoughts. "There is no point for appetisers, is there, Adam? You're addicted to big trouble as much as I am."

There was silence, followed by him breathing heavily into the phone. I don't deny that he was my twin in some ways, but one thing that differed us from each other was that he had no room for emotions, like he was devoid of them. While my medication made me the same way, I knew that I cared. I cared.

"Well, I love Sandra," I said, "and that makes her a part of my story."

"Be my guest," he said and hung up.

A gentle voice behind me uttered, "What's the story about?"

I turned to face Sandra, who looked pale and thin. She was wearing a thick green cotton sweater and skinny jeans. She was wearing her hair down, but her curls had lost volume at the roots. I felt anger for a moment, seeing her like that made me want to fall apart. It took three big steps to embrace her. I dug my face into her hair, hoping the patchouli scent was still there. It was mixed with a trace of disinfectant, which I could smell inside the building.

"Let's go somewhere where we can talk," she said.

We entered the building and walked straight through the hall in silence. She didn't respond to the hug as passionately as I'd hoped, and that had me paranoid about what was coming next.

In fact, the clinic began to look more like a hospice than anything else. It was also larger than

I thought; it had another wing running west perpendicular to the length of the mustard-coloured building. There, a door led to a huge courtyard with small pavilions and garden beds. The narrow walkways were made of paving stones that directed you to every pavilion. Sandra guided me towards the one next to a row of sunflowers. She sat down with a tired smile and closed her eyes as she raised her nose to breathe. I slowly sat across from her on the bench, feeling out of place. I remembered the superiority I used to feel when we first met and hung out, but too much had happened, and I suddenly felt like the complete opposite.

"It's nice here in the morning. It gets really hot at around noon, though," she said and opened her eyes.

The previously child-like face had matured into something motherly and firm. Had I seen her mother earlier, I'm sure they would have looked the same.

"You look like shit, Diane. Did someone run you over?"

She never used to joke like that, and the best I could do was ignore it. When her lips became a straight line, she almost struck me like a stranger. It didn't feel like I only spoke to her yesterday when she called me a psychopath.

"Your dad's a very beautiful person," I said.

She grinned. "Do you want to interview him and fuck him, too?"

"OK, what the fuck is wrong with you, Sandra?"

She closed her eyes and shook her head nauseatingly. "I'm sorry. I talk to you as though I'm talking to my ex," she said.

I didn't understand why she couldn't refer to him by his name already—why she had to maintain that big of a distance. Trust issues befell me. I didn't know what I could tell her. What would she keep to herself? What would she tell Adam? What would make her not hate me more, in case she already did?

"I'm on different meds," she said.

"Since when."

"Yesterday. Hence the coldness. They kicked in pretty quickly. But—nothing will stop me from doing what I'm predetermined to do."

I hated it when she talked like that because she was never the fate-oriented person she'd claimed to be. Only people near death talk this way.

She rubbed her eyes and yawned into her palm. She looked like someone who had just suffered from a nervous breakdown.

"I'm sorry I was such a pain yesterday," she said. "I had this episode and panicked, so I tried to call the people I trusted."

And I let her down. I remember her telling me how much her family loved her and how much they relied on her to be the stronger person within the family. So it didn't surprise me that they were the last people she wanted comfort from. Showing signs of weakness would shatter everything she'd tried so hard to conceal.

"I was born to nurture, Diane. There's nothing I can do to change that. It's the only distraction I have. And if I can't even do that right, then what's the point?"

"Maybe you're not aware that it all starts with you first. Taking care of yourself."

She and I used to talk about self-care a lot, and I was the one who lacked it the most. However, so much more had triggered her current state, and I didn't know how to undo it for her, as I had been selfish.

"I had a little therapy session yesterday," she said. "She said I had this habit of being drawn into other people's orbit and completely forgetting about how beautiful my own can be. But if mine was beautiful, I wouldn't be interested in other people's, right? This is so stupid…"

The lack of self-worth is a common mindset in every person, plus the misconception that they need to find someone to fill that void. If you are not complete on your own, no one will be able to do it for you. I wasn't sure if she remembered me telling her that once. It just felt inappropriate to repeat it, though; I wish I had repeated it. Perhaps her eyes would have lit up, or her lips would've curled into a half smile.

"I'm tired of defining conscience and convincing people they have one," she said.

Again, it pissed me off that everything she said referred to her issues with Adam, but he was right. What did I know about them?

"You never defined it to me," I said.

"You already know it, Diane. I'm talking about people who deny intuition and emotion because they think these sentiments take away self-control."

"But they do."

She looked frustrated and leaned forward, placing a hand on my chest. "Conscience isn't about reason; it's about…"

She hesitated as she looked at me and leaned back against the bench, groaning. We had a similar discussion before about animal instincts versus human conscience, or being human in general, except that I couldn't give a shit, knowing that most people wouldn't want to be compared to animals. Animals weren't born to question or think.

She and I had the best conversations any two friends could ever have, especially with that age gap. I remember us arguing about who would make a better Jesse or Céline. But since I was the one capable of arsehole moves, she christened me Jesse Wallace for fun. I saw no point in creating meaning anymore for something we didn't understand.

Was I the only one thinking about our fun time together?

"What's underneath all that ice, Diane? I could swear there was something."

"Can you fucking quit these metaphors already, Sandra?"

I pictured Pluto's ice shards in its eastern region, so tall they would shoot all the way up into the sky—an army of sharp blades organised by Hades himself. But whoever fell from the sky wouldn't die from a wretched death because they would freeze to death before they even hit a spike.

"I know you're obsessed with Pluto," she said. "Remember when I showed you that article about Pluto's thermal inertia? The way its atmosphere was absorbing heat under the surface? That was around the time I thought you and Jake would turn into a nice pair. It was *hot*. I thought that bit of warmth was sustainable, whether Jake or I initiated it. I really just wanted the best for you."

"You don't get to decide what's best for me," I said.

"I've heard that one before. It's more than what teenage kids tell their parents. We say it to friends and lovers, too."

I had had my chances of spelling out the exact same words I'd told Mr Williams, but I froze the moment she rolled up her left sleeve. She was bandaged from the elbow down. It was the same arm that showed the six-inch cut in the spring.

"Well, the inertia has disappeared," she said, staring at the pavement.

Suddenly all our beautiful moments were funnelled into a dark wine bottle with a long, smooth neck. There wouldn't be any more memories together, but I did hope the existing ones would eventually ferment into something delicate and palatable. Memories have always been stronger than the present, and they sure taste better when you store them away for good.

"Maybe it's better this way," she said and even forced an obligatory smile where the corners of her mouth pointed in different directions. It just wasn't how she would smile. In fact, I didn't recognise those lips anymore.

I'd been feeding off of her hopeful nature and youthfulness for a very long time, and she was done giving. When you know something is over, you know. Emptiness engulfs you. There is a chill in your chest that makes it feel like you are in ice water.

"My parents want us to cut contact."

What did my hunching, motionless body look like to her? It was hard to tell because I hadn't looked at her again that day—even her words began to fade into small echoes or whispers inside a cave. If she were ever to stop talking, I wouldn't be able to find her in the dark anymore or myself.

"I love you, Diane. The time we spent together meant a lot to me. Reykjavik was magical…"

I couldn't tell her that she was also loved. Someone else had to.

A NEW DAWN FADES

FADE IN:

INT. Diane's room

Diane stares into the camera and lowers her gaze.

FADE OUT:

TEXT - WHO ARE YOU, AND WHERE ARE YOUR PARENTS FROM?

FADE IN:

Diane moves towards the iPhone camera and adjusts the ring light behind it. She sits down and exhales.

> DIANE
> I'm Diane Ling, the chief editor at "Broken People of Manchester." I was born and raised in Manchester. My parents are Sheryl and James; they are from Macau and immigrated to England

in the early Eighties. They were
poor, so they travelled to
England by ship. I asked them
what the Red Sea was like, but
they don't remember anything
about that journey.

FADE OUT:

TEXT - WHAT'S YOUR EARLIEST CHILDHOOD
MEMORY?

FADE IN:

                    DIANE
When I was younger, I used to
have nightmares about choking.
Sometimes, I was a foetus with a
nuchal cord, which is having the
umbilical cord around the neck.
I would wake up gasping for air.
My mum never told me about the
birth complications until I was
older. It turned out I did have
a nuchal cord. What surprised
me more was that she had a
prolapse. So when her water
broke, the cord dropped through
the cervix into her cunt. She
knew something was wrong and
immediately called my dad, who
was at work. She started walking
to the hospital, hoping she'd
meet him on the way. Instead,

someone stopped for her and
rushed her to the emergency.
My heart rate had decreased, and
my system lacked oxygen. They had
to aid her through my delivery
quickly. Had it been ten minutes
later, I probably wouldn't have
made it. Dad didn't show up at
the hospital until an hour
later. Does the panic I
experienced during those
nightmares count as a childhood
memory?

FADE OUT:

TEXT - WHAT HAD THE BIGGEST IMPACT ON
YOUR LIFE?

FADE IN:

                    DIANE
I've been on medication since I
was a kid due to panic attacks,
schizophrenia, and bipolar
disorder, among other things.
I'm pretty good at hiding them
when I'm content. Besides
routine and structure, it's
finding solace in other people's
misery. The funny thing is that
I always set them free for good.
But I can't combat my own
anguish. The biggest impact was

falling in love for the first
time and letting it interfere
with my work. I loved Chris so
much that we even planned a
double suicide, only so he would
be free from his demons. But
this is not how you get rid of
demons, so I tried to stop it. I
asked Chris what his biggest
fear was, and he said sharp
objects. So I suggested we'd end
our lives at my father's butcher
shop by burning the place down.
I told him how Dad used to
slaughter ducks and geese by
breaking their necks or
beheading them—how he would make
me watch. So late one night,
Chris and I went there; I passed
him an eight-inch chef knife,
and I disappeared in the back to
quietly call the police. I came
back naked, and Chris was
holding the knife at the wooden
handle with his index finger and
thumb. He looked like he never
even cut vegetables in his life.
I threw my arms around him and
kissed him, and I slowly took
the knife from him. He felt
cold; he was trembling all over.
I could tell he was also mad. He
realised we didn't bring any
jerry cans of petrol, nor did we

have matches or lighters. He
asked me, "Are you trying to
turn this into an Elliott Smith
and Jennifer Chiba story?" I
didn't know what he was talking
about. And as soon as he heard
the sirens, he snatched the
knife from my hand and gripped
my neck, pushing me against the
wall behind the counter. I
smelled the marinated rump
steaks in the meat display,
ready to be sold the next day.
It's crazy how strong your sense
of smell becomes during a fight
or flight. It was a raw moment
where I wouldn't have cared if
he had rammed it into my chest.
He said I betrayed him and that
I was selfish. When he let go of
me, I sank to the floor and
sobbed. He climbed on top of me
and held the knife over me. He
called me a coward, saying that
I never had the guts to do it
myself and that I was using him.
And he was right. I said that if
he didn't kill me now, I'd tell
his husband all about us. But he
charged all that anger towards
himself, not me. He cut his
throat like an amateur and
survived it, and he overcame his
fear of sharp objects. I still

believe that had I not fallen in love and had I interviewed Chris much earlier, I could've saved him. Greg, his husband, never forgave me. Why would anyone?

FADE OUT:

(Black screen)

The sound of a lighter strike, followed by the whooshing of air. Glass breaks in the distance, and the sound of spreading fire becomes more audible.

FADE IN:

INT. TV shows the BBC morning news

                    FEMALE NEWS REPORTER
          An incident of arson was
          committed at Philips Meadow
          Clinic at three a.m. this
          morning.

The TV screen shows surveillance camera footage of a person wearing a black hoodie and a black face mask. The scene changes to the clinic's reception area on fire. Thick, dark grey smoke billows out of the windows.

FEMALE NEWS REPORTER
The perpetrator is assumed to be
a female five foot and three
inches tall. Minutes prior to
the fire, an unknown nurse had
evacuated the remaining five
patients at the clinic. Two
Molotov cocktails were used to
set the empty staff room and
administration area on fire. The
perpetrator supposedly pulled
the lever of the fire alarm
station shortly after. The
police are still investigating
the motive. Only a few months
ago, the mental institution was
charged with abusive behaviour
towards its patients…

The screen changes to the Met Office
weather channel, showing scenes of
large waves wiping out Plymouth,
Bournemouth, Portsmouth, and other
southern cities.

MALE REPORTER VOICE
We're literally being wiped out
right now. Millions of lives in
the northern and southern parts
of our country are gone! If the
water has not reached you yet,
you likely don't give a rat's
arse. Yes, I'm talking to you—
the people in the Midlands. But

rest assured that you're not
safe either. What Sir David King
said about the mega-tsunami was
true. It's about to obliterate
us all, and there will be no
escape, not even for you!

Video footage of the London Shard's
tip above water. Dead animals
floating on the water in the North
Wessex Downs Area. Birds are flying
over the Forest of Dean, which is now
an ocean.

                MALE REPORTER VOICE
Why am I even warning you? Weeks
ago, I told you that a deluge of
rain was hitting the English
Channel. So, why are *you* still
here?

The TV shuts off.

FADE OUT

SHAMEFUL METAPHORS

Suicidal people are capable of anything. But when you have a death wish, it doesn't mean that you're suicidal, as you can be unconscious of your desires. The truth is that I have been fairly content with the things I do—creating distracting meaning to pass the time. But the time comes when you have to stop projecting an idea onto people. I have not been treating them for who they truly are, nor have I given them any credit for their uniqueness. In fact, I hate to see most people for who they are, but when I spot something special that stimulates my imagination, I have to pursue it and make it my own. It's a numbing experience to see things as they are. I'm sick of second-guessing people's intentions, so I've always felt misled in relationships. When you're young, you trust the wrong people, or you attract those who are a reflection of your unconscious self. While the consequences are nauseating, they take you to a dark place where you can feed your imagination and channel your dejection. It has always been my method of escaping the hollowness that people form around me. My creative outlet is all I have, but it's not people that fuel it; it's their story—the perfect type of fiction you'll ever get—because none of it is true once you retell it in your own words. And that's what my readers love about my blog, nothing more.

I open my eyes to Jake watching me. I thought he came back to pick up his iPod; instead, he told me he saw my video and connected all the dots immediately. He recognised me in the news too, which had me puzzled because the police still haven't knocked on my door. They might be too busy with something else that's going on.

"Can I ask you something?"

He brushes his fingertips down my arm and says, "You want to know if I killed Lauren? Do you think I did?"

"Yeah."

He laughs, "OK! Well, I did see my nana in her and strangely enough, that was the reason I got with her in the first place. I never understood why until I realised that it was pure malice."

I sit up and put on my Chevelle T-shirt before he thinks we'll fuck some more. There is something about the term *malice* that summarises all human actions.

He continues, "I treated her very badly. I would beat her, rape her, and use a different object each time to sodomise her. She loved it, all of it. And the more she loved it, the angrier I got."

He stops and closes his eyes for a moment as though it hurts him to replay those scenes in his head.

"I had those severe episodes, too, that I couldn't control. I probably would have killed her if I hadn't dumped her at a mental institution."

I remember him telling me that he'd had some medical treatments done because his medication was no longer working.

"Long story short," he says, "I only did the makeup."

It's pissing outside, but it isn't like the usual Mancunian rain when it's wet and windy at the same time; rather, a tropical cyclone. Water is hitting my windows with such force that it's leaking inside. I'm surprised I still have electricity.

"I love you, Diane," he says, "Please come with me."

"Where to Jake?"

"A bus is leaving for Birmingham tonight…"

I scoff. "I'm not going to fucking Birmingham!"

"Do you even understand the current state we're in? You can't stay here, Diane."

I shrug my shoulders.

"There are helicopters just south of Wolverhampton…"

"Going where? Russia? Mongolia? How do you know you and I are privileged enough to even step on a heli? Don't you know how the government works?"

We're both sitting cross-legged on my bed now like two teenagers arguing about a science project.

"What else do you suggest? You can't tell me you're staying here. The state of emergency is now. More than half the city has already evacuated."

I smile at him, marvelling at his eyelashes as I always do. "OK," I say.

"OK, what?"

"I'll come with you."

As the storm calms, he heads home. He says he expects me to be at the meeting point at half past eleven. If he doesn't see me, he'll come straight back to get me, even if it means he misses the bus. The news has said nothing about the state of emergency; in fact, there is no more news, and the channels are all dead. For a while, the weatherman on Met Office was on air 24/7, but Exeter is no more. Whenever I check my Instagram and Facebook feeds, I've gained more likes than I've ever received. Most of the people I interviewed in the past are sending me their love. I no longer know what it means or if it has ever meant anything. Why are those people still on social? More than half of them will soon be gone anyway. But at least they are in my cloud storage and, most importantly, on my USB. The conversation I had with Adam comes to mind about little things and little bites—all the trivial details that simply don't matter, like us. And yet, I cling to my subjects like they're all I have. I've shared my part to gain their full trust, but even with all of our stories combined, we won't ever shine like an erupting star in the galaxy, and no one will ever care once we're gone. And that's OK.

The streets are underwater. The infrastructure is dead, but I still see people wandering around like nothing has changed. It's the last calm before the big defining storm, and I have no motivation to look it in the eye. Each step I take with my rubber boots splashes cold water against my legs. The air is hot, humid, and salty. I try to call my parents, but both their phones are dead. I reread some of Sandra's old messages, encrypting some more metaphors I believe I have missed. I missed none. Next, I listen to Adam's latest pod, in which he appears to be drunk and ranting about the corrupt society. He's so much more articulate than I ever will be, reflecting my own mind, and I admire him for that. While I still choose to delude myself frequently, he's devoid of any delusions.

It's dark and overcast, and not all street lights are working. As a message from Jake appears on my screen, I accidentally step into a pothole and fall facedown in the water. I get back on my feet quickly and stare at the wet, frozen screen. It's not showing me a preview of the message, and shortly after, my phone dies. Faint voices are coming from Hulme Park, and there is a rumble of engines. I start running.

When I arrive at the edge of the park, I see two motorcoaches and a bunch of people in the distance. They appear to be civil, calm, and courteous. Families with children are among them, too. I also spot Jake staring at his phone. He's wearing a backpack, like he's off on a big adventure. A strong wind starts to blow, and I hesitate to move, realising that not only my feet but my ankles are submerged now. The lights above me are flickering, which catches Jake's attention. Before I take the next step, a figure steps forward from behind the lamppost, and the next thing I feel is a sharp object entering my stomach. All I see is Jake dropping his things and running towards me. His medium-length afro is loosely tied back, bouncing as he sprints.

I look at the person breathing against my face and grab a handful of his hair.

"I'm sorry," I say to him.

He replies, "I wish the double suicide actually happened. I would've been able to move on."

It hurts to breathe, and I fall to my knees. My hands rest on the warm, small handle of the knife, which appears to be some kind of a folding knife. It's nothing compared to the one I'd placed in Chris's hand. I hear Jake charging at Greg, fisting him in the face until he falls into the water. The sound of punches and kicks fills the air until the body of Greg lies there, motionless.

"Diane! Are you OK?"

I pull the small knife out before he has the chance to tell me not to. He starts swearing as the blood oozes through my black shirt, flowing down my jeans. He takes off his wrist scarf and presses it against my wound. I'm still holding the knife but in my unsteady left hand. Without thinking, I find myself pointing the bloody knife at him. He takes a step back, and our eyes lock instantly.

"What is this? Diane?"

Pressing against the wound helps. But no matter how much it hurts, I take a deep breath to maintain my balance and understand what my agenda really is. Then, I flip the knife with my fingers so the blade points at me. I bend my arm and place the tip on my chest. He shakes his head and lifts his hands, mouthing no.

I nod at the gazing crowd behind him. "Go, or I swear, you'll regret it."

He knows I know no martial arts, and he can easily just knock the knife out of my hand if he wants to. For a moment, it's what he intends to do until something dawns on him. Even when Jake takes a step back, I notice how firm my left grip has become. The point of the knife is piercing through my skin. My heart is beating so fast against the knife I feel the throb on the handle. But there is no way this little thing will break through my sternum, so I hold the knife against my carotid artery. I'm more of an amateur than Chris and simply want this moment to end before all I feel is an embarrassment.

"Fucking go!"

"I do know you very well, Diane," Jake says. "And you are no coward. I wanted you to know that."

As it starts to rain, he finally gets the wake-up call to return to his group. He doesn't look back.

"Wait," I say, and before he gets his hopes up, I point at Greg. "Please take him with you. He won't hurt you."

It takes me about twenty minutes to walk back towards the Central Library. The streets are dark, with barely any functioning streetlights left. I shouldn't have gone to Hulme in the first place. Pressing against the wound takes a lot of energy, of which I'm running out. I feel cold, but it helps not to fully acknowledge the pain and freezing sensation, especially because I have someplace to be.

Adam's intercom isn't working, and the main entrance door to the building looks shattered. The reception area is flooded and desolate. I climb the stairs to the third floor and hear shouting. There is light coming through Adam's door, but it's not him that's shouting. The angry voice reminds me of my dad's. I remember being six when I heard my parents argue about me. I feel nauseated and crave some light, so I enter the flat to face the screaming. No one hears me open the door, even as I begin shuffling down the corridor, using the wall as a prop. My jeans are soaked in water and blood, tainting the wall red as I move.

"Dad?"

I take a deep breath to fight the light-headedness. Reaching the edge of the living room,

I see Adam belly down on the floor with his hands tied behind his back. He has a black eye, and his nose and lips are bleeding. He smiles at me and addresses me as "butcher girl." That smile fades almost instantly when he tells me to go. The bright LED lamps on the mantle are hurting my eyes. One of the windows is shattered, and the strong wind pushes the stormwater into the room, flooding the area.

I step into the living room to kneel beside Adam when suddenly Sandra's father walks into the room, holding the thick green cotton sweater that she wore when I last saw her.

"What are you doing here?" he asks me, disappointed. "Are you involved with this piece of shit?"

He looks wild and out of his mind, so in my current state, I don't know what the right thing to say is.

As he approaches me, Adam stretches out a leg so that Mr Williams stumbles and falls. For this act, he earns himself a punch in the face and a kick in the stomach. Adam groans and curls into a foetal position. Next, Mr Williams crawls towards me and grips me by my shirt, unaware of my bleeding stomach.

"Did you know that Sandra saw him a day before she killed herself?"

I shake my head uneasily.

"I don't even know why I told you about it all. I even invited you to the funeral. But you're no different than him. Wait, did *you* send her that audio file?"

I try to look at Adam, who is struggling to get his head off the ground as the water splashes against his face.

"It's all your fault…" Mr Williams says.

The grip is now on my neck, and for a moment, I see my father turning my head towards the reality I do not want to acknowledge.

I reach into my pocket for the folding knife and stab Mr Williams in the neck. He falls to the side, making gasping sounds, but maintains eye contact with me.

"I'm sorry, daughter," he gasps, unblinking until his last breath.

"It's OK, Dad."

All this stress has me bleeding even faster through my wound. It seems like the big wave has already arrived, as the water is filling the room more forcefully. At least Adam's delirious laugh distracts me from the scene and nausea.

ACKNOWLEDGMENTS

I want to thank Gareth, Sam, and Neda. You know why. I also want to thank those who may not ever hold this in their hands, but without their former guidance and mentorship, I wouldn't be the writer that I am today. So, thank you, Elizabeth, Francis, Nikita, Alan, and Nick.

PAULA C. DECKARD was born in Hamburg, Germany, where she grew up. After completing high school in the UK, she attended Goldsmiths, University of London, to study Creative & Life Writing. *Heart Like A Hole* was released in 2018 and is her first book of fiction. *Plutonic* is her second book of fiction.

She loves to connect with readers and writers who appreciate dark literary and transgressive fiction. Paula lives in Canada.

Learn more about her or subscribe to her writer's pages for news, blogs and more:

https://paulacdeckard.com

https://www.terrible-lies.com